BECAUSE YOU LOVED ME..

I DON'T MIND FALLING IN LOVE, ALL OVER AGAIN

BECAUSE YOU LOVED ME..

I DON'T MIND FALLING IN LOVE, ALL OVER AGAIN

Ritwik Mallik

Srishti
Publishers & Distributors

Srishti Publishers & Distributors
N-16, C. R. Park
New Delhi 110 019
srishtipublishers@gmail.com

First published by Srishti Publishers & Distributors in 2011

This is entirely a work of fiction. All characters and events are totally imaginary.

Typeset in AGaramond 11pt. by Suresh Kumar Sharma at Srishti

Printed and bound in India
Repro Knowledgecast Limited, Thane

This book is dedicated:

To both my **grandfathers,** for their blessings, love and those memories of being pampered,

And to **Daksha,** for everything...

"Angels have no philosophy but love..."

~ **Adeline Cullen Ray**

You make me smile like sun
Fall out of bed, Sing like a bird
Dizzy in my head, Spin like a record
Crazy on a Sunday night
You make me dance like a fool
Forget how to breathe
Shine like gold, Buzz like a bee
Just the thought of you can drive me wild
Oh, you make me smile

— **Uncle Kracker**

Acknowledgments

I missed out a few people last time around, so it is time I made amends. Firstly, I'd like to thank my greatest support system and my biggest bunch of well wishers i.e my family. I'd like to send a very big hug to my parents for being the best in the world and my grandparents and all those whom I have mentioned previously or even missed out. I am sorry for that...everyone in my entire family has a huge role to play behind every word I write. I'd also like to use this page to tell my youngest family member, my little niece, Megha that I love her a lot and that maybe someday her uncle will be able to write books that she loves reading.

My family friends in Noida (a big part of it constitutes my neighbours) deserve a huge round of applause for being my immediate family even when I am far away from home. In this case, Samir uncle and Shivani aunty and their two devils Meher and Dhruv need a special mention. Also, Rashmi aunty, Rachna aunty and Nidhi aunty for being the mothers I needed whenever my own wasn't around. I just can't forget their contribution when I was hospitalized ill.

A few of my most important friends, Akanksha, Shriya, Aashna, Piyush, Viral, Apramit, Vartika, Disha, Shreyas, Sarthak, Bonisha, Nandini, Swati, Brij, Sanjay and Antra who have always chipped in with their suggestions.

A big thank you and lots of love to Ashwini for finding time to go through my chapters and 'approving' the content. I could never have done anything without you.

Any acknowledgement wouldn't be complete without mentioning Daksha. By far she has had the greatest influence on my life. She's always there to correct me when I'm going wrong and also there to pat my back when I am doing the right thing. Her words never run short of encouragement and her presence makes me feel 'so-myself'. She is special, she is important...she is the best thing that could ever happen to me.

Srishti (Srish) – girl you rock! I've never seen someone as amazing as Srishti. She is someone who you can't afford to miss talking to even by mistake. Her views are always an enriching experience and it makes you think beyond the limits of your perception. And her perception has always come in handy whenever I needed to back up the *philo* content in the story. Thank You so much!

Also, thanks to a certain Poppy (who wishes not to be named)...who has been the sole reason behind initiating the process of writing this book. And I promised her that I will not divulge any more details.

My readers have helped me grow a lot. I need to thank people like Vasu, Radhika, Poonam, Jeet, Ekta, Nabiah, Yash, Dia, Baabusha, Reema and all those who picked up my book and read it and enjoyed it when I wanted the most. I would never have been capable of writing another work of fiction if it wasn't for your constant pestering and nagging and making me believe that I was fit enough to write again.

Kudos to the entire team at Srishti Publishers for helping me out at most difficult stages of my life and for showing confidence in my work when no one did. I am indebted to you all for life.

Salaam to Sid Sinha and Karan Singh Sawhney for being nice buddies when I needed them to help me tackle criticism. And just not care a &%$@ to what people felt about me.

I need to thank my school-mates Himanil, Mayank, Uday, Saral, Mihir (dada), Karan Malik, Riddhi, Akash, Ritu, Radhika, Mridul,

Mimansa, Nayantara, Amartya, Sahil, Tanya, Samad, Navya, Aditya and Sajili (I remember what you asked for).

My evergreen teachers need to be thanked for my evolution of a C-grader in writing to a guy good enough to get published. A new inclusion to the list of teachers who've had a positive impact on my life is Gurleena Ma'am. Thank you very much.

Tejinder Ma'am also needs mention for those brain storming sessions of Eco classes at the end of which I find my knowledge to be at a level higher than before.

I'd like to end by thanking everyone in the beautiful city of Noida (and Gr.Noida) who have done so much for me in the past four years. From the rickshaw waale bhaiyyas to the one at the cyber café who gets me print outs for free…every one of them need to be credited. I must mention my auto driver ji, Shamsher Singh who waits for me for long hours, not complaining and not charging a penny extra and helps me cover small distances without taking any pay.

And last but not the least, I thank the entire family of Delhi Public School Noida…I love you all!

Friends Meet

7th October, 2016.

Ritesh Garg entered the elevator of the Centre Stage Mall, Noida. He pressed the 3rd glowing button from the top and the elevator started rising. "Third floor", the recorded voice said. Ritesh stepped out. Impeccably dressed in casual attire, Ritesh gave the impression of being a high school dropout. His ruffled hair and rim less spectacles added to his persona of what was deemed to be attractive but not so handsome.

Entering the Ruby Tuesday, it took him minutes to locate his best childhood buddy, Pallvinder Pandey.

"Oye Pallu!" he raised a hand and shouted.

"Abbey O Ritu!" Pallvinder excitedly reacted.

With the energy of a fifteen year old, Ritesh quickly took a seat next to Pallu. On his other side, sat Pallu's girl friend, Saniya.

"Meet Saniya," Pallu said proudly.

"And you must be the one and only...RITESH GARG! The one who redefined love!" Saniya made an expression close to that of fainting.

"Yes, I am indeed that foolish idiot." Ritesh smiled meekly.

"Not at all...!" Saniya gazed at Ritesh. He felt a bit uncomfortable at first, but later on things fell into place.

"So how come you have remembered me?" Ritesh sipped some water.

"Don't ask! For the last 4 months Saniya has made my life impossible..." Pallu said.

"...she wakes up and takes your name, goes to sleep and takes

your name…she's crazy over your book." He added.

"My book? You mean the one I wrote eight years back?"

Pallu nodded. Saniya kept on gazing.

"So that's why we met? Cool! You sounded desperate when you wanted me to come from Gurgaon immediately!" Ritesh signaled for the waiter.

"Yes, yes! And we are planning to get married – she won't marry me unless she finds out what happened." Pallu seemed paranoid.

"What happened? Erm sorry didn't get you."

"Arre Ritesh…what happened after your first book got over?"

"Yeeees…." Saniya sung and continued gazing.

Ritesh whispered the order in the waiter's ear.

"How should I know what happened?" Ritesh raised his arms in surrender.

"Naughty fellow…why joke?" Saniya asked.

"It's a thing of the past, why do you want me to talk about it again?"

"But, it is indeed an integral part of our life…" Pallu caught hold of Ritesh's hand.

"…mere bhai, please – I want to get married soon. Please complete your story and give me a taste of glory. Pleeease!" Pallu plead.

"Ok – ok…fine, since you are so desperate to prove that you are not gay, then fine – I will tell you the story!"

"Yeipeeee…" Saniya jumped and pushed the glass.

Luckily it was empty or else it would be an encore of the watery conversation, Ritesh thought.

"So where do I start?" Ritesh asked.

"Where you left....!" Saniya said.

"Ok, I will start my story from March 2009. Couple of months had passed by, since Aaru and I broke up. The memories were still new and the wounds were fresh. I had decided that I would study sincerely and an acquaintance in the form of Manas had made things even more lively...charsi sala...ha ha ha!" Ritesh laughed his heart out.

Pallu held Saniya's hand under the table while Ritesh, made himself comfortable. He started narrating while the world ceased to exist...

Prologue

"Okay, so this is it," I exclaimed.

"This is what?" Manas asked.

"Sector 34!"

Manas looked at me disillusioned through the flock of hair falling on his face, covering his eyes. The visible traces of his pseudo intelligence reflected well within the depths of those green rubies that God had gifted him with. A tattered green blazer, clumsily knotted tie and an ID card hanging down from one of his trouser loops added to the description of one of the most callous yet fun-to-be-with personalities I had ever met.

He was as old as me but his behavior was that of a seven year old stuck inside the body of a sixteen year old. His stiff resistance to the bouts of claustrophobia that came with the requirements of being a growing adult who seemingly had to show signs of responsibility and maturity in thought processing, came in the form of slapstick humour which he used to his benefits most of the times. But somehow or the other, I found his jokes to be lame and low in content.

With playfulness in his actions, he kept on licking the remaining traces of the butterscotch milk on his Cornetto.

It was an hour back when I had met him on the Metro being bullied by some of his seniors in school – when I had swiftly intervened and got him out of the sticky spot. Spending a few hours with him made me feel that I knew him for ages. "You are addicted aren't you?" He asked.

I raised an eyebrow. "Addicted to your mobile," he replied.

"And why so?"

"For the past half an hour I have been noticing that you are either texting or surfing Facebook on your phone, quite strange for a person like you – who supposedly does not have any girlfriend,"

I gave him a tired look. The mention of the word girlfriend brought me back memories of Aaru.

"You are such a *charsi*," Manas scowled.

"Charsi?" "Yes, charsi..." he said.

He continued after a brief pause, "*charas*, my friend is a drug. And the one addicted to it is a *charsi*."

It was quite surprising to me that an acquaintance would start calling me names on day 1 itself. And this was one of his super lame jokes that I had been hearing over the past hour or so. My mind quickly rushed back to the first one he had narrated with great poise. It was something like – 'what will happen if no water remains on Earth?' And the answer followed, 'People won't get to swim!'

It was for courtesy sake that I had laughed. Now I question myself on whether his joke was aimed at testing my intellectual capabilities or was it Manas at his best.

"Why are we here *charsi?*" he asked.

"In search of a tutorial for myself," I replied.

"Hmm..." he nodded. "And what am I doing with you?"

"I just saved your ass if you hadn't notice. So it was evident that you had to tag along with me. And also it is a matter of coincidence or rather *bad luck* for you that we both live in the same Sector and unknowingly haven't met ever since time existed. So, if it isn't too much of a hassle for you – kindly stick along till I reach *Orientation* and then we both can go home together."

"Orientation?"

"Yeah, it's a tutorial run by Paritosh Gupta. Quite famous..."

"But there are a 101 tutorials near our place, why Sector 34 all of a sudden?"

"Because it is the graveyard of my puppy love..."

"Graveyard of what?" he asked, all confused.

"...my puppy love," I said as I got lost down the memory lane.

It had been exactly been two months since I had broken up with Aarushi – the love of my life. It had all started off as a bad case of acne, high energy hormones and a strong dose of infatuation in high school. I fell in love with her for no reason as such and then things grew deep and we soon started being addicted to each other.

It started off with wooing a girl who had a crazy family consisting of an even crazier mother. The motto of her family was simple, score 99, take up Science – enter Medicals or Engineering and then go for arranged marriage... *life will never fail you.* Talking to a guy other than your brother was a crime and getting a mark less than the desired 99 could end up in death penalty. But I did finally manage to convince her.

After hours of phone calls and hundreds of texts – she was mine. But, that was seemingly the easier part. Holding on to the relationship which everybody thought was nothing more than *bullshit*, hiding it from our parents and sustaining on a life full of compromises, adjustments and meeting demands was really easier said than done. But we did it, we held on to our relationship for quite some time before something really disastrous happened.

A phone call to her already confiscated mobile at 4 AM in the morning sealed the fate. Her mom intercepted the call and after a little bit of pressure on a girl born with idealistic thoughts cracked her down. She revealed everything, including the details of our conversations and then nothing existed any more. I hung on as long as I could and took every bullet of insensitivity shot at me but to no avail. She broke up and I was all alone.

Did she ever love me? Does she still love me? Were some of the questions that existed in my mind. The path to understanding who decided what and who did what was long and winding.

And I thought being in Orientation would benefit me hugely. It overlooked Durga Housing Society and a certain House no. 125 where my *angel* lived. I loved her a lot...I wanted her to be mine forever, but now there was a mountain to climb.

Aaru and I were in Class X. The board examinations were 11 months away. The society would kill you if you couldn't crack the boards and somehow it held more importance to Aarushi because of her family's great history of producing Einsteins.

When a child is born, a lot is said about his education and this was *it.* Class X – gossiping aunties, old uncles, retired army men and relatives who don't even remember your name...every bloody person was interested in your marks. *"Kya loge? Science?"* is the question they'd often ask. And we, the students at the bottom level of the food chain sustained everything. Coaching centers made humongous profits, teachers unleashed the beasts within them, the income of photocopying shops doubled but we had to write pages after pages – day after day, crumbling under the load of deadlines, peer pressure, parental expectations and acceptance by the society.

On top of that I had my falling grades to look after and an emotionally disturbed girl to win back...

The History of *'Charsi'*

It was a Tuesday, and it had rained a lot. I guess even the Gods had cried the day I was born. They knew it very well, the crime they had committed of sending me and my sinister plans to this holy planet. Nevertheless, a community of people was happy of course and it was my family - my sweet, loving family.

I was a caesarian! According to my mom, right from that moment I was lazy and even lazier. So what my dear doctor did was that she pulled me out of my comfort zone – and on that very day I realized how mean the world is; they bloody well don't want you to relax!

I cried a lot (more than the Gods did - no idea though). My dad was patrolling the streets, full of nervous energy as usual constantly puffing away and blowing out smoke rings. Cigarette was a stress buster he believed and the number of stressful items in his life would increase from that day on.

So as I said, I cried a lot. The entire street heard it, perhaps the entire city did. No wonder, the sound of my tears (a sign of unhappiness) was a cause of worry for the City of Joy.

I was born in Calcutta, now Kolkata! Rightly the City of Joy. My family was one of the earliest settlers from the *baniya* community from Uttar Pradesh in Calcutta. There was a myth that the grand dad of my grand dad actually offered funds to Job Charnock, poor me…myths remain myths!

My Montessori schooling was done from a school called *The Tree of ABC*. Strange how people came up with such names – but yeah, it was actually a *nice* school. This school was located at a walking distance of five minutes from my home.

So on the first day, I remember quite vividly how mother had cuddled me out of bed earlier than usual. I had no idea what was going to be done with me, and like every day I agreed to whatever she said just the way, prisoners listen to their jailors.

My grand dad drove me to school that day on grand Fiat automobile. It was sky blue in color and had this strange gear which stuck out from the side of the steering wheel. Well this system seems weird now but was quite trendy fifteen years back. The number plate read: WBF 9898. And after 13 years pondering over the number plates of millions of cars, I still haven't come to the conclusion about their significance.

A young lady of my mother's age stepped forward to hold my hand and take me away from my mother. Mom thought I would cry, so did grand pa…but guess what? I DIDN'T! Instead, I turned around and sent both of them a round of flying *pappis* before accompanying my teacher to my classroom. My mom's eyes were watery, at that age it felt weird why a lady would put water in her eyes while coming to drop her son at school – now I think differently.

We studied in a make shift classroom as Archana Ma'am (the young lady) told us. And in that very classroom: I fell in love for the first time!

'Tude dekha toh ye daana tanam, tyaar hota hai teewana tanam – ab yahaan te kahaan jaye hum, teri tahon me mar jaaye hum!'

I started singing at the top of my voice when Sanjana smiled at me. I smiled back and balloons exploded in my heart. I asked ma'am whether I could share my crayons with her. I was very nervous thinking that ma'am might refuse and forgot that my bladder was full. The moment she said *yes,* in sensations of respite – I loosened my bladder and was swimming in my own *susu.*

Sanjana looked at me from a distance and started laughing. I looked at her and started laughing at myself. We kept on looking at each other till Nilima di, our attendant – crazily dragged me away to clean me.

So that is how, began my first love story…

Every morning, I pestered my mother to dress me up faster and had all of a sudden lost my lazy touch. I finished my milk faster and completed my *potty* time faster. Mom was surprised at my new found speed; she thought it was the impact of going to school. Partially, it was the impact of going to school and *falling in love.*

I reached school five minutes earlier than Sanjana every day and raced into the premises without giving mom and grand pa a last look. I hurried to my class, dumped my bag and then waited for Sanjana to arrive. When she arrived with the attendant, I would wait for the attendant to leave. And then, I would approach her and press her cheeks and leave a peck on them.

Sounds funny now, she used to laugh and smile and then giggle a bit. Then she used to run away. And just the way, I would be doing things in coming years; it was Montessori where I learned how to turn situations into my favour. With great caution, I would open Sanjana's bag, take out her crayon box and then hide it in mine. End of each day I would return it.

This meant that ma'am would ask me to share my box with her and then we would sit next to each other and talk gibberish. In days to come, Sanjana realized that I was the one who took out her crayon box – but she never said a thing. She too had fallen in *love with me*!

We learnt counting 1 – 20, then 1 – 50, and then 1 – 100. We learnt how to count backwards and forward. We then learnt alphabets, A – Z. I scribbled the letter *S* in my notebook. It looked like *5,* so no one bothered. And by the time, I could write *My name is Ritesh and your name is Sanjana...* My father got transferred!

My love story came to an end; it was my longest affair till date, which lasted for two years. No longer would I hide her crayon box, or cuddle her, or kiss her. I was far, far away in a jungle called *Noida.* A concrete jungle it was!

When I was twelve, I tried Googling the name *Sanjana Sharma.* The results were 95,100. I gave up hope and switched off my PC.

The search for new Sanjanas...began...

Puppy - Love

"C'mon Ritz, don't tell me you seriously liked her?" Sonali giggled.

"Obviously!" I replied.

"Uffo, *kya yaar* – that is not possible! You are a *baccha*. This love-shove isn't good for your health," her tone seemed patronizing.

I took in a deep breath and let go of it slowly - And then concluded my dramatic pause with a sigh.

"Ha ha ha…" Sonali started laughing, gasping for air in between.

"Once you finish please tell me…" I was seriously annoyed that someone was not taking me seriously.

"Ha ha, no yaar, ha he he…why angry? Ha ha he…you seriously, he he ha ha loved her?" Her laughter was incontrollable.

"SONALI!" I shouted.

"RITZ!" She shouted back.

"Sonali?" I inquired.

"Ritz?"

"Listen NOOOO!"

"Tell NOOOO…….HA HA HA HE HE!"

"I am hanging UP!" I threatened.

"HE HE HA HA….OK OK OK…"

"…wait Mr. Garg, give me a second. (deep breath) Yes tell me now!" finally Sonali was ready.

"I still like her, does she like me?"

"It depends…"

"Depends? What the hell depends? Answer me CLEAR CUT for god's sake."

"Hmm…what do you feel about her?"

"Aaaah….nice question, I feel…"

She interrupted, "But wait a sec, don't say anything from your God damn brain, do it from dil se…you know, every time you try speaking using your brain – you end up giving me PHYSICS LECTURES!"

"Okay!" I agreed.

"When I look at her, the world ceases to exist. Her eyes and her beautiful smile. Her lips and her dimples, her long hair and graceful self….aaaaaah it melts my heart!"

Sonali was badly trying to control her laughter. I could feel that very well.

"You know what's the problem…?" She asked.

"If I knew that, wouldn't I have had solved it myself? Go on tell me whether she likes me or not, I mean as in STILL likes me?"

"Ritz, are you sure she ever LIKED you?" "What if it was a big drama from the start?" She fired two questions.

The answers were difficult. I knew very well that Sonali understood me like the back of her hand and she would understand my feelings without me speaking a word.

The lump in my throat was dry; I wanted to gulp but that sound would still be heard. The answers bore the marks of the harsh truth. Maybe Aarushi never liked me; maybe it was just to keep me content. I didn't wish to think in that way, it made me senti. I never wanted to believe that she didn't like me…the very moment that thought crept into my head – I started having bouts of nausea. All the shimmering hope seemed to be getting lost and with that seeped away my happiness.

"I-I don't……know! I don't know." I replied in a morose tone.

"That's why you are wasting time thinking about her rather than doing something concrete." She said.

I kept silent.

"Ritz, *meri maano toh* just move on dude. You are at your best when you flirt, pass comments on girls' figures, fight, play….uuuuuuuuh dunno what else. But yeah, you should try to make it a part and parcel of your life and you know…"

"…Yeah, I know Sonali. Your friend must have told you to convey this message right?"

"*Nahi yaar.* Aarushi will not do anything like that…uffo try to understand – she's helpless. Did you forget Radhika auntie…?"

"O. How can I forget her, *ek auntie ko dekha toh aisa laga jaise aaru ki mummy jaisc meri saas jaise uncle ki biwi jaise Aryan ki mummy jaise haathi ki ho eeeekkkk bitiyaaaaaaaaaaaan o o o oooooooo*!"

All of a sudden I had this spurt of happiness and started singing an old Hindi song with improvised lyrics.

"STOP! STOP! STOP! You ARE KILLING ME!" Sonali shrieked.

"Okay!" Everything felt silent.

"Honestly, Ritz…don't be so mushy. You get me?"

"Mushy?"

"Arre over-senti and too much of feelings. You are in a board class…study dude study."

"…you bet Sonali!"

"Gosh, you never told me not to be mushy when I filled my first book with senti quotes??!"

"Actually, I didn't have any words to describe your love story…it was….uh…not getting the word…" She spoke in a hushed tone.

"What word?"

"Arre to describe your story yaar!"

"O!"

"it was like…..hmm likkee…..yea! Gotchit!" Sonali sounded excited.

"What?"

"PUPPY LOVE! YOUR LOVE STORY IS PUPPY LOVE! HE HE HA HA. SHOW SOME head dude! Don't be a devdas for god's sake. Flirt and try out new jeans, it is in your genes."

The word 'jeans' in our group was used for 'girls'. A top secret codeword it was!

"So Sonali, are you trying to insult my love story by calling it puppy love?"

"No. Just saying the truth. Show some maturity…when I mean maturity I don't mean your hairy face or your baritone, I mean think big dude."

"I wish I can argue Sonali, but seriously – I have given it all up!"

"O my lill shona pona friend, no need to give up hope. You are special…"

"Am I?"

"Yes."

"But why?"

"Because, Aarushi had been asked out by so many boys before you. So many of them had fallen for her looks but it was only you, who she chose, and that makes you special!"

"I feel better Sonali…what can I do to have her back?"

"What she asked you to do…!"

"She asked me not to waste my energy on unnecessary things."

"Then don't!"

I begged to differ. I chose silence as my answer.

"Thanks for your time, see you."

"Toodles!"

She hung up, so did I. I had loads to think about.

In hopes of securing proper marks, I left my house (for four hours) in a search for good tutorials with a mad hatter called Manas. He constantly irritated me by calling me charsi but yeah, he was nice at heart.

The story continues from Sector – 34, a place where it all begins again…

It All Begins Again

'DURGA HOUSING SOCIETY'

The name plate read. The name seemed familiar, but the hoarding didn't (as it had been printed quite different from the hand written one, three months back). It had been over, three months since I last visited this apartment. Pallu had fallen ill with chicken pox and Radhika auntie had warned me from setting foot in her auspicious apartments. Mom was crazy with my Class IX passing marks and dad had restricted my computer and mobile usage. My phone had a meager balance of rupees three and my pocket had seven more than that. I was walking past the apartment which was the year before, my second home. I had never ever felt so miserable while visiting Sector – 34 like I felt now.

The smell of food in the air threatened to block my nostrils, the road threatened to push me towards the racing cars, the entrance to Durga Housing sent across terrorizing vibes. And the poor guard who was staring at me in a state of daydream suggested that any moment he would get to know of my past.

Like before, my throat went dry and eyes went watery on remembering my beautiful past. O! Beautiful days they were, when I raced across the entire city on my cycle just to reach this place within seven minutes. When I stood below Aaru's balcony with lover boy looks and a heartwarming smile, when I waited for forty minutes at a stretch just to see her at the balcony waving at me…

"How far is it from here?" Manas asked.

"Uh, just two minutes, I guess…", I looked around searching for the placard on one of the trees which would give me direction towards ORIENTATION.

"Must be around…here……somewhere…aah there it is," I pointed towards a house at the far corner - just a few meters away from the second gate of Durga Housing Society.

"And what do you plan to do?" Manas asked.

"Study of course!"

"Study? You will study?" he chucked away cornetto wrapper.

"Yes, study!"

"And me?"

"You can give it a try. You would be requiring tuitions wouldn't you?" I asked with a smile.

"Ritesh, try to understand – I know you are interested in meeting your exporter, but please don't behave like an extremely over dosed charsi!"

My phone beeped instantly. It was a message from Pallu. It had vaguely something to do with Aarushi. As a result of her name's mention – my entire attention got diverted to the mobile and not what lay ahead of me.

And then,

BAM! I collided with someone who was walking towards me, and that too with great force.

My head twirled and I could see proxima centaurs all around. Registering the thought, that I had hurt someone badly – I looked around to locate an injured person. After a frantic search for that injured person, when I looked up - all I saw, was a cross and angry girl looking at me. Her stance was fearsome. She had her hands on her waist and her hair was all askew. Her head was bruised but she was in no mood to seek sympathies. Rather she wanted to tear me into chunks of meat.

She continuously looked at me and I continuously looked at her. She was tall, as tall as me. Strikingly fair and had hazel eyes (just like me). Her long brown hair rolled down her shoulders and hid her lovely eyes. The girl was of my age perhaps, her features suggested. She was of slim built and was wearing her school uniform.

We were still staring at each other unable to take the initiative of saying something. I tried but was thoroughly unsuccessful in doing so, I guess I mumbled something like, *excuse me I'm sorry,*

And eventually what came out of my mouth sounded, "*So use me I'm sexy!*"

...

...

"You-you-you-you-you!" She shouted at me at the top of her voice.

I looked at her, strangely not retaliating for a while.

She kept on repeating you and then shaking her long fingers in front of m eyes.

"Sista! Don't get stuck on *you*..." I had to point out that she was repeating the same thing.

"Uuuuuh!! YOU-YOU-YOU WILL TELL ME THAT???!" Phew, I was safe from yodeling *yous*.

"I guess I did," I scratched my head looking at the ground.

"YOU-YOU-YOU, egregious, feeble minded, bogus boned, smutty head, blind, cock eyed, screwed face, long nosed IDIOT! HOW DARE COULD YOU BUMP ON TO ME?"

"...but, but I was..."

"JUST SHUT UP!"

"Ok?!"

"YOU ARE ANSWERING ME BACK?! HOW DARE YOU-YOU-YOU know WHAT YOU DID?"

"No..."

"AGAIN?!"

"OOOPS! Sorry, I forgot." There was something about her that made me feel stupid to be answering her. There was this innocence in her voice that suggested that whatever she was doing was actually a put on. She was really not angry as she wanted to portray.

"YOU-YOU-YOU, egregious, feeble minded..."

"...sorry to interrupt you, but you have completed that list already..."

"Don't put in YOUR ONE LINERS!"

"Okay..."

"You answered back again?"

"Yes," I nodded my head in disapproval.

"No, I mean." I nodded in approval almost immediately.

I was confused.

"Now, will you apologize or keep on STARING at me??" She bellowed.

"Stare…!"

"…um…apologize…"

"I mean stare and then apologize….I mean only apologize!" I bit my tongue.

"Then do it fast…" She started tapping her feet.

"Do what?"

"Say SORRY!"

"Why do you want me to say sorry, for no fault of mine…?"

"YOU-YOU-YOU…" she started off.

"Sorry *meri maa…* sorry sorry sorry – ab please please DON'T START-START-START OFF again! Please!" I folded my palms and begged before her.

"I know you boys very well! *Battameez lafangey*! You deliberately bump onto girls…my mom will put you behind bars! I will make sure…that…"

Manas in the meanwhile was nowhere to be seen. Being coward that he is, on seeing me encountering a problem – he ran for his life. And now, I desperately needed to find him but before that I had to get rid of this whining girl.

"…if you don't mind," I said. "I will talk to you later about this? So AUNTIE, I will take your leave now…!"

I saw the drastic change in her expression. The word auntie struck her badly. And after all those wonderful curves, no wonder she was angry when I called her an auntie!

I turned around and started moving in hurried steps.

"YOU-YOU-YOU, I WILL SCREW YOU!"She chucked a shoe at me.

"FOR THAT YOU NEED A SCREW DRIVER…" I shouted back.

"URRRGGHHHHHHHHH!!" She was in a fit of rage. Her voice suggested.

I saw her jumping up and down on the same spot. Boy! Was she angry!

I wanted to piss her off a little bit more and for that I had to be at my flirtatious best, I turned around and sent her a flying kiss. Not waiting for her reaction, I moved on towards *orientation!*

Orientation

'Orientation – Resolution for a Revolution'

The board outside the entrance tilted at an angle of 85 degrees looked unimpressive.

The staircase leading us to the classroom in the basement looked even more unimpressive.

By now, I had envisaged the probable outcome of Mr. Paritosh Gupta, an IIT Roorkee pass out, the one with the key to my future, the one with whom laid the answers to my problems in Bio, headaches in Mathematics and heart aches in Physics. He too, I thought would be the most unimpressive.

I walked in casually with Manas.

"Ch-ch-ch-ch-ch-ch……" Manas was making peculiar noises.

"Chup bey! Can't you see we are in an institution…? Impression counts IDIOT!" I whispered fiercely.

"Ch-ch-ch-ch-ch-ch-chaaaarrrrsi!!" he hissed back.

"F......."

"COME COME COME...."

Oh God! I thought. The very moment that giant sitting on his giant chair started ushering us by saying 'COME COME COME...' – the first thought that came to my mind was that it was his daughter that I had messed up with a few moments back. Then I realized that her petite structure was very dissimilar to this man's huge belly. Then another thought rushed in to inform me that perhaps all the lunatics and the escapees from asylums resided in Sector – 34. Because all of them had this creepy ability to repeat a word thrice! But that thought too was unsatisfactory as my angel was no lunatic! (Although her mom was)

By God's grace, in a matter of seconds I understood that the repetition of words was just to personify the speech of the giant!

The giant's amazing English accent struck me at once, and I can only do justice by spelling out the words as he pronounced them.

"Please take a sheat (seat)!" he graciously lifted his heavy bottoms and pushed a couple of chairs towards us.

"Sir, as you know..." I began.

"Yes, yes. I know that you have come for tuitions, I know that you are weak in Maths and Physics...I know you need assistance but for that I have to, when I say have to, I mean I have to give me introductory speech; so may I?" He completed his sentence in a hurry.

I glanced at Manas and he glanced back at me. Then both of us with abnormally large eyes looked at the giant. So he was PARITOSH GUPTA!

He was short heighted, grey haired and carried a heavy load in his stomach. His Charlie Chaplin moustache made things even funnier.

He wore a tie with red polka dots on it and a white shirt, black trousers and sandals added to his strange get up.

He looked to be coming from a wealthy family, where all the family members starve because of his eating habits. He smiled at us and shook our hands.

He was relatively fair and had puffy fingers. He straightened his tie and cleared his throat.

"In such type of a tutorial uich [which] provide education in quality to ishtudents, I expect a littal [little] contribution from the ishtudents [students] aar [or] their family members. Revolution for a Resolution....oho Resolution for a Revolution I means! "

He showed his teeth again. We smiled back. Nervously we spoke again and in fifteen minutes left that place with a couple of forms in our hands.

"Charrsi..." Manas spoke. We were taking a rickshaw back home.

"Yes?" I said grumpily.

"Did you notice something...?

"What?"

"While you were talking about your he he he ha exporters of charas he he...I was observing bhooka aam's desk."

"Bhooka aam?"

"Arre I know you are too much into addiction, but come on – couldn't you make out that Gupta guy can easily be called a BHOOKA AAM!"

"O! Continue..." I was seriously not interested in his sense of humor.

"Yes, so as I was saying…I was saying that…what was I saying charsi?"

"You were talking about some great observation…" I replied.

"Aaaah! There was this form on that Aam's table…"

"What form??"

"IDIOT! SHUT UP! And listen!"

"Ok."

"There was this filled up form which had the picture of a very pretty girl."

"Ha ha ha he he ha ha …don't tell me that you have a crush on her!"

"NO NO! You never know, I might. Actually that's the reason I have decided to come to this tutorial even though this Aam will be teaching me!"

"You are going to study….that too for a girl??? IM-POSSIBLE!" I laughed.

Manas brushed his hair, "No charsi, she was REALLY pretty!" "And you know what, it's guaranteed now that she will be attending this tutorial cause I saw the payment options ticked and her parents' signature wagera wagera…"

I started singing, "Pyaaar hua ikraar hua…"

"Got to know anything else from the form? Phone number? Address?"

"Yeah, I glimpsed at the address…but…saale…charsi…naam to pooch pehle!"

"Oh haan, yeah, tell me what's her name…and then kahaan rehti hai woh bhi bata de!"

Manas cleared his throat just the way Mr. Gupta did.

He touched his chest on the left side and spoke in a poetic manner, "Aarushi my looooovvveee, I will come to meet you at DURRRGA HOOUUSING SOCIETY!"

"WHATTT???! DID YOU SAY????!!" my jaw dropped. There was only one pretty Aarushi in Durga Housing Society!

Manas didn't reply. He looked at me dumbstruck. He was expressionless.

I had a long story to tell…

My first day!

Manas took out his notebook and started scribbling on it. In between he made a forgetful expression and stared at the ceiling – a rusty fan hung from there. After few minutes of observation he went back to his scribbling. After long moments of acute irritation, the time had arrived for me to lose my temper. The more I tried not to pay him any attention, somehow or the other his stupid gimmicks caught my eye. I was just praying that someone came by and relieved me from this torture.

We were waiting in the so called lobby of Orientation – *road to success.* The bloody basement doors were locked and we couldn't get in neither could we stand the fishing heat outside. March sucked and so did Manas. Call it coincidence or not, both started with murderous M!

"What are you doing, my dear?" I turned to look at him.

"Counting…counting ch-ch-ch…!" He laughed in between.

"Cut the crap," I replied.

"Yeah, cut the charrrrsiii!" he ran his hand through his uncut hair.

"Manas…!"

"Riiiiteeeeessssshh…" he replied almost immediately.

"Bata na, why are you looking at the fan? For what" I had to pass time.

"You know what?" Manas got up.

"What?"

"…I think, I like Aarushi. I do charsi…"

"…and I think, I will propose to her today itself when she comes." He looked out for my reaction.

"Nice idea." I said after a pause. "Do you want me to celebrate?" I asked again.

Deep within the very thought made me go dry. I could imagine Manas and his mowgli hair, Aarushi and her beautiful smile, standing all alone on a lonely street. I couldn't take it any longer.

NOOOOOOOOOOOO! I wanted to scream, I wanted to run around, I wanted to jump off the EIFFEL TOWER…

But hey! Wait a sec, why? It was just a freaking thought wasn't it?

But it still was SCARY!

I avoided the thought with great difficulty and tried to look at something other than Manas.

Turning around, I saw a number of faces - both familiar and unfamiliar. I was seeing many of them for the second or the third time, as I quite vividly remembered by detours to Durga Housing Society most of last year. There they were, the ones standing in front of me – some would walk around talking on the phone while others would make quick escapes from their tuitions; most of them were casting me nasty looks, perhaps thinking the same.

And then, I received a gentle push from someone behind me, it was a soft touch. "Sorry," the voice apologized for accidentally pushing me. I would not have turned around if it was not for that voice, it was familiar, it was sweet and it was heart whelming.

In matter of moments, I was looking into her eyes – her long lashed beautiful blue black eyes. *"It's okay"*, I said in a soft tone. I was mesmerized by her face. It was the face, I wanted to see.

Her reaction was different; she quickly withdrew herself on seeing me. The color faded away from her face and a certain gloom descended on that charming appearance.

"You?" she asked.

"Angel…I mean, umm…umm"

"Aaru! Aarushi!" she replied. "Yes, Aarushi…" I said.

"…you here?" I acted as though I knew nothing of her being present.

"Dad put me in a couple of weeks back, surprising to see you here." She was wearing a pink colored shirt and blue denim. I thought she disliked the color pink, but on second thoughts – who am I to know about it anyways, we were together for only three months weren't we?

"So?" I asked.

"You have followed me here as well?" she replied in a questioning tone.

"I guess, you have!"

"No, I haven't! I had no idea that you'd be here…" "Shit! I'm all messed…" she was ruing her wrong decision.

"It's okay Aaru, m not here for you. I am here for studying, get that." I tried to sound as convincing as I could.

"You'd better be, because mom will not be in a good mood when she hears this."

"HELLO! Ask your mom to take a hike, why the hell is she troubling me for?"

"Listen RITESH, don't talk about my mom in that tone – you have troubled me and my family for the past six months and I guess it's time you STOP doing so…!"

"Wow! Now I AM at FAULT? Bullshit…!" I shouted out.

"Yes you are and you always will be, and now stop talking to me, sir has arrived." She said grumpily.

"Bhookha aam….!" I made a bad expression while others greeted him. Thank god I was mumbling and he didn't hear me well enough.

I rammed the pencil onto my desk and broke it into two. The un-chiseled and rugged portion scratched my fingers. I licked the bleeding skin.

"No need…thanks", Aaru said.

She was just sitting behind me. Gupta Sir was yet to distribute our question papers when I heard Aarushi asking for a pencil from her neighbor. I wanted to be the one to give it to her, but she didn't take it.

I cut my fingers and it was stinging badly. I sucked the blood, the pain stayed on.

"You should have told me that- would have saved me the enjoyment!" the sarcasm was evident in my voice. "Will surely remember from next time." She answered mercilessly.

How could someone be so mean with someone as sweet as me? I asked myself in disgust. I had no idea regarding the amount of poison related to me that Aaru was fed with. Her mom seemed to have done a very good job.

"Attention, Class tens: place your name on the left hand side of your paper and your roll number on right...blah blah blah" the *bakwaas* continued as Gupta Sir shouted at the top of his voice.

I paid little attention as tiny drops of blood dirtied my paper. I checked my pockets frantically but didn't get a handkerchief. I was a sure goner. I could very well imagine my ray diagrams of convex and concave mirrors to be beautifully designed with red polka dots, just like on Sir's tie on day one.

"Take this!" Aaru threw her handkerchief at me. Like an oasis of love for an affection thirsty animal, the handkerchief (with sunflowers on it) made me turn around instantly and apprcciate Aaru's kind gesture. There was a lot of hustle and bustle – just before the papers were being distributed and it gave me those extra few seconds to put in my words of gratitude.

"Thanks Aaru..."

"Anytime."

"I know you are my friend, you don't need to act." "You are not any friend. Even if someone on the streets is injured, I will help him out."

"Agnes...the angel whom everyone loves..." I smirked.

Aaru's expression went blank within moments. At first I thought she was humbled by being compared with Mother Teresa. Then I thought, maybe she was late to react on my sarcastic humour. Then I thought that the word *angel* might have offended her.

But when I turned around, my thoughts changed.

My nose was poking into a soft pillow. The pillow was covered with blue stripes. It was making groaning sounds; the more I poked it with my long nose. I gradually increased the angle of elevation of my eyeballs when I met a pair of it's cousins.

Those cousins of my eyeballs looked at me with a lot of exhaustion.

I guess Paritosh Gupta was tired of asking his students to *shilence pleashe!* As a result when the *Romeo and Juliet* of his class were having their sweet discussion (irony). He wanted to intervene.

"Ishtand (stand) Up! BOTH OF YOU!" He shouted.

Both Aaru and I took three seconds in total to respond to our stimuli. Sir's voice sent jingles down my spine.

He caught me by my side locks and looked at Aaru menacingly while I was crying out in pain.

Troubles Galore

"Aaru…I'm sorry!" I pleaded.

"Don't be!"

"But…but I was at fault wasn't I? As in, look at me at least!"

"Look at what?"

I was surprised at her reply. Now what did she want to take a look at?

"Me?" I asked.

"Yeah yeah." "…why not! What's so interesting huh?" she sped ahead.

I ran faster. She took a right turn, so did I.

"…my apology!" I said.

"I don't need it…throw it in the dustbin."

"How?"

"Uggggh! As you wish, just stop stalking ME!"

"I am NOT stalking you…" I said as we reached the entrance of

Durga Housing Society.

"Yes you are...and for your information – I have reached my house, so please leave me alone..."

"...before I fall into more trouble, because of you – Ritesh!" she had tears in her eyes.

"I will, I will...just once – accept my apology, please!"I stressed on the last word.

She stopped all of a sudden and turned around sharply. I was about to bump onto her, we were saved that it didn't happen – God knew how many miles I'd have to walk to get an apology then.

"Listen carefully. Paritosh Sir..." she began.

"Bhookha Aam!" I put in my word.

"SHUT UP WILL YOU?" she barked.

"Sorry...continue..." I replied.

"Listen. Paritosh Sir has let go off me with a warning. This is our first day and thanks to my lucky stars nothing happened. But something could..."

"What could happen?" I saw no logic behind her sentences.

"Everything could. People could know, sir could know...mom could be called; your mother could be informed. Our parents would have met, there would have been un-pleasantries...God knows what NOT!"

"Chill, will you??! Nothing of that sort has happened!"

"But it could have! Why take a chance?"

"But the problem started because of me didn't it?"

"Yes!"

"Then, just a small acceptance of apology and problems solved *yaar*!"

"Fine! Is that all you want?"

"Yeah!"

"It's ok! I have forgiven you...now just leave!" she smiled artificially.

I smiled back. I guess both of us turned back at the same time. I moved in slow steps as a Honda Accord swiveled past me.

It took me a few seconds to understand from where the sound had come. But when I turned around, I went numb.

The car had hit Aarushi and she was lying there in a pool of blood.

The very next thing I remember doing was to pick her up (with a lot of difficulty and with no assistance from the passersby) in my arms and run in search of a hospital.

A Ride

Those three minutes would turn out to be the most defining moments of my life. The world knew how much I loved Aarushi, my friends knew how much I loved her; but maybe I didn't know how much I did.

She was in my arms stirring. I covered her wound and moved forward – my shirt draped in blood.

In spurts, thoughts started creeping up. Maybe I was late in reacting. Maybe I was wrong in asking an apology. I was the one who followed her and distracted her. It was cause of me that she lost crucial reaction time. Why didn't the Honda hit me?

Pushing myself from the gaze of onlookers – a filmstrip started to roll in front of my eyes: those blissful moments when I first met her last year, when I narrowly escaped dangerous traffic to win a bet, when I lied to see her standing cross at the balcony, when I stayed awake all night speaking to her; all started to reappear.

I wanted to kiss her forehead, maybe this would be my only chance.

Once she'd be in her senses – it'd be quite difficult to explain my feelings. She would never understand me. I fastened my steps as the thought of something misfortunate happening crept upon me.

The incident had left me numb, but I had firm control over my emotions. The very thought of a misfortunate outcome made my throat dry and created an enormous vacuum in my heart.

Luckily, a *guardian* appeared as I was making my way through the market. It was Manas. And maybe for the first time in my life – I was glad that he was present.

"Charsi, charas over?" he said.

"Can't you see this is something serious?" I hissed.

"Yes."

"Then?" I expected a solution.

"Then what? I know that my parents are doctors but doctors don't reproduce hospitals, do they?"

"I know that ass!" I said impatiently.

"Then what do you want to know?"

"How do I take her to a hospital??" I spoke hurriedly.

"Oh! You mean this girl with ketchup all over her face?"

"Mind it Manas! You ARE pissing me off!"

"O O! My apologies…let's take her on a rikki!"

"Rikki?" I was dumbfounded.

"…rickshaw! That's the quickest way!" he was all excited.

"Then what are we waiting for, let's go…"I said hurriedly.

"Chalte hai! *Abbey o ricksha*!" he shouted out at a passing rickshaw.

"*Babah re babah…pulish kesh hai (police case hai). Nahi jayenge.*" That rickshaw puller shouted out.

"Aarushi will lose precious time, if we keep on asking – Manas please do something…"

"Wait charsi…wait…I won't let your addiction die." He winked.

His humour was intact even at times of crisis. Aarushi was my addiction – he knew it.

Running up to a rickshaw puller who was digging his nose, Manas did something strange. He pushed that person in a fit of rage and that poor malnourished guy fell down thanks to his light weight and Newton's law of gravity. Even in a fallen state, the guy appeared clueless to why he was being attacked.

"*Abbey kaminey! Kutte! Mera wallet chori karta hai!* Huh??!" Manas started shouting at the top of his voice.

"*Rickshaw mei BAITH ke wallet chori karta hai!*" he kicked him.

I understood his codeword; he wanted me to sit on the rickshaw. I did so without delay.

"*Ab dekh tera kya haal karta hu mei! Tu jaanta hai mera baap kaun hai??!*" Manas continued speaking.

The puller nodded in disapproval.

"*Nahi jaanta?*" Manas clarified aggressively.

"*Nahi sahib…*" the guy was dusting himself, visibly shaken.

"*Main bhi nahi jaanta…!*" Breaking into wild laughter and throwing his wallet on the fallen guy'sface, Manas ran like a maniac.

At first, it seemed that he was making a run for his life. But it was to the contrary, at tremendous speed he ran towards the rickshaw, caught hold of the handle and pushed it. In a way, this accelerated it and before reality could strike the puller: Manas was on the rickshaw, riding my *angel* to safety!

To the Hospital

"Yeippe!!" I shouted in ecstasy. Aarushi was responding although not fully in her senses.

I patted Manas on his shoulder. He slowed down to respond.

"Happy charsi?" he asked.

"Thank you my friend…a hug for you once we get down." I said affectionately.

"Yuk! Yuk! Saala GAY! Stay AWAY from me!"

I smiled back in glee.

"By the way, would you mind getting down and pushing the rikki from behind?"

"But why…?" I could now stroke Aarushi's hair. I guess by the look of it, she didn't know on whose lap her head was rested.

"…because my legs are tiring. Hospital is near…but still!"

"Dumbo! How can I leave Aarushi on this seat and push?"

"Why?" he asked.

"What if she falls?"

"If she falls…" he paused. "…we will pick her up again!" he said it as though it was a matter of fact.

I made an expression which he missed.

Obviously he would, he was looking ahead!

"What if the rickshaw guy gives us troubles?" I asked.

"I gave him my wallet didn't I?"

"How much was in it?"

"Seven rupees."

"Oh! That's quite a sum." Saying this I kept quiet for a while.

"Even if he does trouble you…just give me a ring."

"Thanks dude! You will help me out won't you?"

"Get down from seventh heaven…I will come definitely. But not to save you *but* to see your ASS kicked, ha ha ha!"

I showed him my middle finger. He missed it.

How?

He was looking ahead wasn't he?

"Hospital aa gaya charsi…" he applied the brakes.

We stopped near *Shri Ganesha Hospital.* The Gods seemed to be following my *angel,* first Durga and now her son *Ganesha!*

What fun! I thought.

Without wasting much time, I rushed into the casualty ward: there was soft music that went on in the background; I let it soak into the tense atmosphere.

Jai ganesh jai ganesh jai ganesh deva…

I prayed that my *angel* would be safe, for the time being I had to send a message to a worried mother, who better than Manas to do that for me!

Riteza to the Rescue

"What is Aarushi's father's name?" Manas asked.

"Kunal." I replied.

"Good. Now what about your addiction? Has she been admitted?"

"Yes, the docs are looking after her...she's got a cut in her head, it's being stitched."

"And what about the formalities? Are they complete?"

"Yes, I told these people about your dad. I think he's a visiting doctor here. And a quite famous one," I said.

"See *charsi,* my dad is FAMOUS!"

"I agree. Now, Mr.Manas...will you please inform Aaru's mom? She suffers from high blood pressure and must be panicking by now..." I paused. "...I don't want her to strangle Bhookha aam for not ensuring the safety of her daughter." I chuckle after finishing the sentence.

"Okay! Wait charsi...give me your mobile and let me speak."

I passed him the mobile. He dialed the number from my contacts. The phone was on loudspeaker mode.

"Hailo!" auntie shouted from the other end.

"Hullo…asaalam waalekum!" Manas said.

"What?"

"saalam alekum…Kunal is there?" he spoke in a hoarse tone.

"No. Who you?"

"I, myself – Mohammad Riteza Wahidullah Rahman, I need to speak to Kunal right away!"

Slightly shaken up by the name, auntie kept mum.

"Reply in the NAME of the GODS!" Manas said dramatically as though it was a religious sermon.

"I, his wife Radhika speaking. You tell." Auntie tried conjuring up sentences.

"So be it! Kunal's daughter Aaruni…" I kicked Manas immediately. "…I mean Aarushi is gravely injured!"

"WHATT!??" there was a terrible scream. I could hear Aryan's inquisitive questions from behind. Even aunty had kept the phone on loudspeaker I presumed.

"Where is she?" she shot a reply.

"Inshallah! Mohammad Riteza Wahidullah Rahman has brought her to Shri Durga…I mean Shri Ganesha Hospital."

"O! Thank you Mr. Mohammad Riteza…erm…"

"…Wahidullah Rahman…ha ha!" Manas completed the sentence.

"Yes, yes…Wahidullah Rahman…ha ha!" she copied him.

"Worry not; your daughter is being looked after by the doctors.

Inshallah – she will be safe!"

I heard a Jai shri Ram from the background. Aryan was already praying.

"O may God bless you Mr.Mohammad Riteza Rahman…"

"…WAHIDULLAH RAHMAN!" Manas roared.

"Will you be anywhere around the hospital?"

"I might. Why?" Manas said quickly.

"Because then I would have got something for you. You have saved my family, do tell me what you want?" she seemed generous. Thank God she wasn't offering her shoes.

"I want your daughter…" I said hurriedly forgetting that the phone was on loudspeaker.

"WHAT?"

"I want doughnuts!" Manas exclaimed, saving my ass. He added, "…mind you, they should be only from M.O.D."

"So be it…!"Aunty replied.

"But….but…my sister Sheikh Namita Hasina will be present to collect the doughnuts on my behalf." Manas looked at me and winked.

"…and remember that she might be dumb but she isn't blind or deaf!" Manas added.

"And what does your sister do? Mr.Mohammad Riteza Wahidullah Rahman?"

"Sheikh Namita Hasina is a nurse at Shri Ganesha Hospital. Any doubts?"

"No…no not at all…do ask your sister to look after my daughter till I arrive."

"Yes, he will…I mean she will." Manas looked at me and winked again.

"So when will you be coming?" Manas alias Rahman asked.

"In ten minutes."

"I stole a rickshaw while getting your daughter. You will find that puller creating *hungama* in the market place. Do pay him off and tell him that your son will return him the rickshaw."

"Ji ji…" auntie replied not surprised at the fact that an unknown random person knew that she also had a son. Quite stupid she was at that moment of time.

"Sheikh Namita Hasina will be waiting for you. Khuda Haafiz." Manas disconnected the line.

"Who is going to be Namita Hasina?" I asked inquisitively.

"You will charsi. Get ready to dress up like a nurse."

"But why should I?"

"Cause only then can you stay close to your angel!"

"But what if her mother sees me?"

"She won't recognize you. Do me a favour will you?"

"Yes. Surely."

"Ask that nurse to get you a spare set of their uniform and get ready quick. I will be back with a very essential disguise for you."

"What?"

"Medium sized watermelons! See you charsi!" he winked and left in a hurry.

What the f**k! I told myself. *Watermelons?*

Nurse Namita

As promised, Manas got the watermelons on time. Supposedly, the vegetable vendor had given him discount on hearing that he required watermelons to save someone's life.

The nurse had given me a set of spare clothes and an ID card. I put on the watermelons and looked at myself in the mirror. The overcoat seemed fine, I had shaved earlier that day – my face seemed fine. My walk would be okay and since I was dumb, I didn't have to think too much about my voice. So the only thing that remained was my hair as they were too short. The possible solution to that problem came in the form of a nurse's cap.

I was briskly escorted to room no.413 where Aarushi had been accommodated. Due to the impact of the collision she had – she was made unconscious. After gaining consciousness, she fell asleep because of thc tircdncss; hcncc shc had no cluc about thc pcrson who had saved her.

She looked even more tranquil and serene when she was asleep.

Her eye lashes were resting peacefully and behind them lay her beautiful eyes. The eyes I longed to see over and over again.

I went closer and touched her forehead. I gently ran my hand through her hair. I held her hands for a couple of minutes and then slowly and gently I bent down and placed a tiny peck on her cheeks. "Get well soon, my angel..." I said.

There was some commotion outside and within minutes, Radhika auntie in her fearful self barged into the room. That jackass of an Aryan followed her closely carrying a bag in his hand.

"Aaru! My daughter!" she shrieked like those mothers in C grade Bollywood films.

She threw herself on top of her and Aarushi woke up with a start.

"Whoa! What happened??" she exclaimed.

"My daughter! Thank God! You are all right...!" she caught her daughter's face and covered it all up with wet kisses. Aaru's expression suggested that she didn't like it even one bit.

After all, my gentle peck was extraordinary.

"Hi Di!" Aryan spoke.

"Hey champ! Who told you guys that I was here?" Aaru asked, happy that she was with her family.

"Some Mohammad Riteza Wahidullah Rahman!" auntie said joyously.

"Rahman? Who is he?" Aarushi inquired.

"He is a savior...!"

"But...the last thing I remember was that Ritesh was apologizing...!"

"That scoundrel...don't take his name!" Auntie tightened her grip of Aaru's hand.

"MOM! THAT HURTS!" Aaru shouted as auntie's long nails made an imprint on her hand.

"Sorry sorry!" "Hasn't that rascal learnt his lessons? Why was he following you? He must be the one who hit you!" Auntie stood up ready to pick up the gauntlet and declare war against me.

"No mumma…I agree he is a rascal but he wouldn't stoop to that extent." Aaru said.

I coughed a bit, informing them of my presence.

"O! You must be Namita Hasina!" Auntie ran towards me, I got nervous.

She held both my hands and shook me violently, my watermelons moved out of place and I caught them and prevented them from coming out.

Auntie found the gesture to be in bad taste. She withdrew immediately.

She turned around and headed towards her daughter's bed, "Your brother asked for doughnuts…here they are!" "ARYAN!" she barked.

Like an obedient pup Aryan came to me and handed the doughnuts. I touched my face and double checked that the mask was placed.

"So, what now? How many days does my daughter have to stay here?"

I gestured my index finger towards her.

"One?"

I was dumb so I nodded my head.

"So be it!" she said.

"I think the visiting time is over so I'll leave now. My husband will be here for the night. So, I better go back home and inform him. Till then, take care of my daughter. And send my regards to your brother." She added.

I nodded again.

"Aaru beta…" she bent down close to her daughter's ear and spoke something in their native tongue. I didn't understand a word. In the meanwhile deciphering what the mother-daughter duo spoke, Aryan casted me nasty looks.

I felt uncomfortable fearing the revelation of my identity.

After long moments of uneasiness, Radhika auntie bade her daughter goodbye and left. Aryan tugged along closely.

It was time for me to leave as well. I was sure that my parents would have started worrying by now, although I had texted them about my friend's accident – they still didn't trust me completely.

Aaru was reading a magazine when I tried to tiptoe out of the room without letting her know.

"Wait Ritesh!" she said.

I stopped on my tracks. I didn't move an inch.

"Disguise was good but not good enough to escape my eyes." She spoke softly.

I turned around in self disgust. Her magnificent eyes which I loved the most spilled water over my plans.

"The moment I heard the name Riteza, I understood it was you. It was quite foolish to dress up like that"

I stood in silence.

"Can't hide your identity from me can you?" she asked.

"I guess not." I gulped down the lump in my throat.

"And thank you for saving my life. If it weren't for you, I'd be with my grandma by now."

"What did you expect me to do? Run away on seeing you in such a state?"

"No stupid." She giggled like old times.

"Then?"

"I knew you were filmy. But certain things about you are not surreal like the world of cinema."

"Trying to flatter me? Go on and list them." She understood my worth finally. I was trying to be dead serious and created an aura of importance surrounding me.

"Hmm...your heart and it's never ending love for people. I doubted them at times but I regret doing so."

"So?"

"Maybe you will forgive me someday for mistrusting you."

"You bet Aaru, I will." I smirked.

"When will you go home Ritz?"

"When you allow me to Aaru..." I said arrogantly. Strangely she kept on smiling.

"Do you know something?"

"What?"

"I am leaving this place...for good."

"Where?"

"Calcutta..."

"The city of joy? For what joy? Made a Bengali boyfriend have you?"

She giggled, "No...no – dad's office is shifting head quarters there."

"So when do you leave?"

"*Abhi toh* I have around 6-7 months."

"So what about your boards?"

"Don't worry – I will leave only after I finish my boards…*papa* is leaving early." She smiled innocently.

"Ok." I said in a prolonged murmur.

We kept staring at each other for some time till things got uncomfortable. The moment it did…I started scratching my head, playing with my feet and cracking my fingers. On the other hand she kept on staring at me.

"Thank you!" She spoke softly.

I looked at her for a moment and didn't speak a word. So she would be leaving me – yet again and this time…I don't know, perhaps the ends would never meet.

"See you later, take care." Not casting another look, I left.

Ritesh's phone rang. With a quick glance he received the call, "Excuse me." He said.

"Sure sure…go ahead," Pallu and Saniya started talking something amongst themselves.

"Oh hi! I have already reached CSM. Where are you?" Ritesh spoke on the phone.

"Oh no! You are stuck in a jam? Damn the Delhi traffic…anyways come fast." He followed after a pause, presumably after the reply had come from the other end. "Bye" he disconnected the line.

"Sorry…" Ritesh said.

"Arre nah nah! No formalities…" Pallu clarified.

"But why did you behave so arrogantly?" Saniya casted an angry look.

"Where?" Ritesh replied.

"Arre! When Aarushi had softened up, you could have used the situation to your benefit. Why did you run away like a coward?"

"Because I didn't have any choice, did I?"

"But still…you could have pacified her! And she would have agreed. Trust me!" Saniya spoke with a concerned look.

"No no! I knew she wouldn't have, after all you can't ignore the daughter's promise can you? Remember?"

"Yes that freaky old promise that she would stay away from you and blah blah…"

"Exactly!"

"Then how were the turn of events like?"

"Exciting…" Ritesh rubbed his palms remembering the past.

"Really? What did you do? Landed with a helicopter on her roof?"

Saniya mocked him.

"Nah! Nah! Didn't have money to rent a chopper, or else would have done that too."

"Aaaw!"

"Jokes apart, I started leading life normally. As in you know, fake enjoyment."

"Fake enjoyment? What's that?"

"Laughing when you feel sad, drinking at a young age and hanging out in friend's place till late are a few examples." Ritesh replied.

"Oh! So you gave up on her?"

"I never did that…!"

"That's amazing! So what are you waiting for…?? Please continue!"

"From where?"

"Hmmm……" She started thinking.

"Okay! It's been a week after she's been discharged from the hospital…" Ritesh continued with his story.

HRD Strikes Back!

It was recess and we were detained. 'We' comprised of Narayan, Sanjay and me. And what was our fault?

When we ought to have been studying the Rectilinear Propagation of Light, we were passing around a joke book titled: 101 Raunchy Jokes.

Narayan had bought it from a railway platform on his way to Kota where he was going to fulfill his IIT dream, but somehow received a rude shock when he realized that there were people more brilliant than him out there. So just to find means of diverting his frustration, he sought shelter in the joke book that filled him with erotic fantasies as well as provided that elusive laugh.

"Physics *ne toh maa ch*** di,*" he scowled.

"Yes, this motherfu***** dog left us with so much of work to do, I told you – we should have played the 'asset realization game', we wouldn't be caught." Sanjay added.

"Yes you are right," I said. "Asset realization would indeed be a

better idea, we just had to sit and rate people's assets and that's it."
"True. But what if that dog came and saw those amazing fractional representations like 8/10, 4/10...what would be our explanation? Eh?" Narayan defended his idea of passing the joke book around.

"Sirjee...refractive index!" Sanjay laughed out, we joined.

"Narayan, go get me some food would you?" I threw the change that was lurking in the comforts of my cotton trousers.

"*Bhen***** - can't you go yourself?" He abused.

"Please yaar, jaa na...!" I pleaded.

Visibly irritated, he got up and left.

Sanjay and I were the only ones in the class.

"How many questions to go?" I asked.

"Seventeen in seventeen..."

"Seventeen in seventeen? What was that supposed to mean?"

"Asshole," he commented. "Seventeen in seventeen minutes...that's like doing a 9 *monther* in one day!"

"Ha ha...funny!" I said.

"I have an idea," Sanjay's eyes lit up. "Just wait and watch."

He scribbled something on the header of his answer sheet and made an arrow to indicate something. He further made criss-cross lines all over the lower half of the page and scribbled something next to it in a box.

It read:

Questions 1-12 below →############# (scratch here to find answers).

"I am done," he got up in a sense of self achievement.

"What the fuck?"

"Yeah..let's submit this," he wanted to do it fast.

"We'll be detained for a week Sanju…" I tried explaining.

"Exactly what I want…you know the chick named Sunaina?"

"Yes," I nodded.

"I want to make out with her. Need your help."

"Sorry, I can't help you in *making out.* That's something a guy and a girl do privately – not something collective, unless and until you wish for threesome." I was getting irritated.

"C'mon, I love her…like I know where to draw a line of course."
"I don't support too much of physicality in a relationship dude, earn her or suck your thumb," I got up to leave.

"Aren't you submitting your answers?" He asked.

"Of course I am. Just going to get some extension and you?"

"I have my masterpiece of course…" he waved his sheet in front of me.

I sneered.

Next thing I remember was facing the flat nosed Physics teacher.

"Extension?" he asked.

I nodded. "Attending marriages lately have you?"

"No Sir."

"Then why?!" he bellowed.

"Sir, other teachers especially the Chemistry sir piles us with work every day. Not easy to list down the valencies of almost all elements on the periodic table."

"You are in tenth. It makes or breaks your life, if you don't study now then when would you study?" he frowned.

"Give me an extension for a couple of days Sir, please."

"Students these days I tell you. Girlfriends, Facebook, movies, malls, pizzas and hamburgers – ask them to study and they want extensions. And then these freaks these days…" he chucked a newspaper on my face. "…these freaks these days come up with weird ideas of making their already easy life easier. How will they survive in the real world? And then we say: *nothing can happen to this generation*, bloody youngistaan!"

I rubbed my cheek which was now red because of the force with which he chucked the newspaper at me. I read the headlines: **HRD Minister seeks educational reforms. Will target board exams.**

A smile lit up on my face, the thought of educational reforms was a joy of relief for all of us facing this excruciating trauma. The haughty picture of the old man with hair as white as snow lit up the moods of a million students all across the country.

I got the extension but Sanjay got badly beaten up. He returned to class with a bruised cheek mumbling things like *corporal punishment*. But not one of us paid him any attention. I had circulated the news that perhaps we might not be having Boards this time as it could be replaced by an internal evaluation system. This resulted in a victory roar that shook the entire school and as the news spread from class to class and the newspaper changed hands…the hopes of a brighter tomorrow for all 10th graders became stronger and stronger.

Trigonometric Woes

"Settle down class!" Amit Laharry shouted at the top of his voice.

"Today, we will start off with Trigonometric identities and trigonometric ratios of certain complementary angles. So class, are you ready?" He screamed energetically like those DJs in the night clubs.

Laharry a new entrant to our teacher's zoo had no idea what life had in store for him. All those amazing years of teaching experience at some Saint school had made him God amongst our group of lazy, laidback, crazy and disinterested teachers. On day one itself, I observed Basu giving Laharry dirty looks. It was sure shot a case of insecurity but when I found out that Basu and Laharry were *chaddi* buddies and had spent their entire childhood in their ancestral village in Bengal promoting homosexuality – I had laughed my lungs out.

Our group of friends was content with the fact that finally we were saved from Basu's constant touching business of girls and boys as he had got a perfect companion in the form of Laharry for all those under the table stuff.

Laharry resembled Johnny Lever. The only difference was that he had tufts of hair coming out above his ears. He seemed fine with his walk and talk so unlike Basu, but the only thing we detested was his ear cleaning business in between class. Although we had a very few classes with this new specie but had estimated its possible outcome, seven weeks and Laharry turns into one of those creatures in our zoo!

"Are you ready?" He screamed again.

"Aiyyo, yes sir!" Shaleen Lama replied. He seemed to have taken some protein shake before coming to school as he was the only one who was *ready* ...God knew for what?

I turned around and checked the total strength. We were supposed to be having thirty seven students, out of which five were unfit. One was in the toilet since the first period (bad stomach) and another had been called by our Principal for carrying 'A' rated magazines. Negating these seven no hopers, we were supposed to be having thirty students. Surprisingly, call it Laharry's charm or the muggy weather out there – there were seventeen students present i.e two more than usual.

"And where have the children gone?" He asked.

"Such a lovely day, bright and sunny – you should open the windows and let the fresh air rejuvenate your soul and body..." he started dancing, just the way he used to in that Saint School – I guess.

He moved towards our class windows and opened one of them with a huge push – call it pressure variations or his freaky bad luck, with a huge *huff and puff* the air blew onto Laharry's face. The free gifts that the air got were a few pigeon feathers and huge amounts of pigeon waste.

Coughing like a lunatic, he shut the windows. The class was so bored of f**king mathematics that they found this seemingly funny incident quite boring.

"Okay! Since the children will perpetually be late for class, today Amit Laharry will *not* wait for them. After all as they say – their loss is *your* gain."

Licking his finger tips and picking up the chalk he started scribbling something on the board. There was the movement of chairs and the students were back to studying. He wrote 0,1,2,3,4. Then he divided all of the digits by 4. After that he placed a root sign on top of them. "Does anyone know what this is?" He was trying hard to energize the class.

"Aiyyo! This toh is the trigonometric ratios of sin 0 sin 30, sin 45, sin 60 and sin 90 saaar!" Lama rejoiced.

"Purrfect! Mr.Lama!" Laharry clapped.

"Now since you already know that cos is complimentary of sin – you start reversing the values and wholaah you get what you want to achieve…isn't this like magic?" Laharry's mouth was watery, excited at the thought of his knowledge.

"No sir! I guess as far as I know, this is like *mathematics*." I said.

"Cocky, Ritesh but intelligent", He winked at me. The class laughed.

"Thank you sir!"

He stopped abruptly and started cleaning his ears again. He took out his fingers after six seconds and started looking at his findings carefully.

"Concentrate…" he shouted still looking.

"Aiyyo…where sir?" Lama exclaimed.

"Here, here…I mean there, there…" Nervously pointing at the board, he cleared his fingers off his findings and resumed his non sense on board.

Our assignment questions were being discussed and solved on the board when I heard Aarushi's friends whispering something to her. I tried to catch a glimpse of her but her friends were blocking my view. Of what I could gather, they were having discussions regarding the newspaper article that had come out the previous day and whether it'd have positive or negative effects on the students. I strained my ears to catch onto stuff like how Laharry is biased and how badly he has checked Aarushi's paper because she was absent for a few days due to family commitments which had not gone down too well with Laharry.

However, I was fearing the worst as Aarushi started saying stuff in her defense quite aggressively and soon her voice was clearly audible. As expected it reached Laharry's ears and….

"AARUSHI!" he bellowed. I swiftly turned to look the other way.

"WHAT NONSENSE??! " He shouted again.

"Sorry sir…" she said meekly.

"You have committed a crime by not paying attention in my class. Instead you were discussing about a stupid article…*you duffer.*

"Excuse me??! How you dare use such language, sir, I might complain against you!" I unknowingly stood up and shouted.

"You might?! Huh? Might? Ha ha! I HAVE THE *might* of the school and the entire management! Get that you Mr. smarty pants! And by the way…who the hell are you?" He menacingly looked at me.

"That girl is a disaster in mathematics…9…7…6…5 – this is not my phone number but her assignment marks out of thirty. And you say that I shouldn't call her a *duffer?*"

"So, if she is weak in Mathematics…it is your job to teach isn't it?"

"Don't forget you are talking to Amit Laharry…Laharry from Saint…blah blah blah!"

"Sorry Mr.Laharry from Saint blah blah blah…I will *not* talk properly!"

Now all the attention had been transferred on to me. I could see that Aarushi was sobbing away as her friends huddled around to comfort her. Seeing her miserable 'cause of this jackass gave me more courage to say whatever shit I wanted to.

"OUT!" he pointed towards the door.

"Are you sure?" I asked. I had no respect for him and I didn't care.

"Wait for me OUTSIDE! I will arrange a meeting with Mr. Martin." He rubbed his palms.

I walked out of the class like a hero. Forty pairs of eyeballs followed me as I made my way out. Today, I had taken a stand against this pigheaded teacher; tomorrow someone else would. I wasn't scared of meeting Martin, the principal either. He was a jolly good fellow. Before I stepped out, I swiftly looked at Aaru. Her eyes were all red and she was still sobbing silently.

You will pay Laharry…you will!

Shrey Calling

"Come in." Jacob said in a hoarse tone.

Laharry walked in with his limp. He took off his glasses in a state of anger and exclaimed, "Sir…this boy," he caught hold of my arm and shook me as much as he could. "…this boy committed the profound crime of interfering when I was dealing with one of the dumbest girls of his class!"

He continued, "Ritesh Garg literally abused me and spoke in a very rude tone. He treated me like his servant and I…Amit Laharry from…..blah blah blah ….will not accept this sort of behavior!"

"Amiiit!" Jacob stood up.

"Calm down…calm down…" he tried to comfort the image bashed Laharry.

"But principal sir…this man is lying – I know what I did and I very well know what he did…" I tried to explain. Jacob raised a hand and shut me up, "you will not ridicule or disrespect a teacher in my school. Headmistress ma'am has been very liberal with you and that is the reason why your wings have come out."

For a brief moment, I made a survey of the room. On all the trophy cabinets that were placed, I could locate the numerous trophies I had won for my school in so many interschool competitions. After doing so much, least the principal does is to insult me by saying that *my wings have come out.* On top of that he keeps shit teachers like Laharry and thinks that he has done the right thing.

"Master Garg," Jacob called.

"Yes?"

"Apologize to Mr.Laharry, immediately. Or else I might have to take strict action against you."

"Sir…sir…but…"

"…no if no but, just APOLOGISE!" Jacob asserted himself.

Fine, I said to myself. I will concede the battle to Laharry but I would win the war.

I turned to Laharry and said as politely as I could, "I am really sorry sir…"

"Ok baccha! It is ok. But do remember not to mix with *duffers* like Aarushi. You are bright and intelligent and you have a long way to go. This is Amit Laharry from…." He started off again.

"Ok then. Both of you, off you go!" Our principal, Jacob pointed towards the door.

After I stepped out of Jacob's office, I turned to Laharry, "Sir, I promise that I will never ever misbehave with you again. And I also promise that I will never ever trouble you."

Laharry looked at me impressed. His chest was puffed up, full on with pride. He smiled in admiration.

"Yes Asshole! Be impressed…puff up your chest in self admiration

cause you have no idea how much I will trouble you in days to come…you have no idea!" I wanted to say all of this on his face but I made do with a wry smile.

Time would tell about Laharry's sufferings. I had a plan…a master plan!

That night, I tried calling Aaru thrice. Twice her mom picked up and once Aryan. Every time they did, I disconnected the line thinking that maybe the next time Aaru would pick up the receiver. Aaru's mobile had been confiscated quite some time back and now I had no other alternative other than to wait for school to resume on Monday. Only then would I get to speak to her.

That very evening, I had met her at Orientation. She seemed disturbed most of the time. All that had transpired in school didn't seem to have gone down too well with her. She was constantly distracted while *Bhookha Aam* was teaching and as a result rather than keeping an eye on the board – I was keeping an eye on her.

Our seats had been separated and were made to sit at two different corners, but still I didn't mind. As long as I could see her clearly…I wouldn't complain much.

I picked up my mobile yet again and dialed her number. Just before I could press the CALL button…my phone started ringing.

It was Shrey, a classmate.

"Hullo!" I said.

"Hey! What sup?"He replied.

"Recollection of thoughts is going on. What about you?"

"Arre, forget your freakin' recollection…guess what?"

"What? Hooked up with another girl?"I asked him something which was very usual.

"No no…mom and dad are out of station. I am all alone in this palace of mine. I called three guys from school for a night stay and yes – my latest girl friend is also coming. You interested?"

"Are you crazy??! Have you seen what time is it?"

"Just 10.30. Night is young." He chuckled.

I was in two minds. I wanted to chill out a bit on the other hand I had to study. At that point of time chilling out seemed more appropriate so without thinking much, "Yes…I can come but…"

"But what?" Shrey asked.

"How do I leave my house at 10.30 PM? Mom and dad will kill me!"

"Arre don't you worry, just stuff up your bed with blankets and pillows. I will wait outside your balcony on my bike. You can come down the service staircase cant you?"

"Yes…fine meet me in fifteen. Chao!" I disconnected the line.

I had little idea that that night would be the spiciest night of my life.

Where's the Party Tonight?

Shrey's house was truly a palace. Coming from a middle class family, I had never imagined that people could build something as magnificent and palatial as Shrey's house. There were fourteen rooms spread over three floors. The servant's quarter could hold up to fifteen servants. There was a private gymnasium and a billiards room. His dad was some big shipping guy and often held his meetings in a board room right next to his work area.

This was probably the first time I was visiting Shrey's house. His room was triple the size of mine and had everything that possibly a teenager could own: Wii, PS3, a huge LCD TV, the best home theatre system and an amazing laptop. I felt jealous for a moment.

Present in his room were: Sanjay, Ashish, Narayan and a familiar face. I was shocked to see her all of a sudden and so was she. Our meeting was quite some time back but I still didn't forget her. It was that same girl with whom I had a confrontation in Sector 34. "Meet my girlfriend, Tia," Shrey introduced.

"Hi Tia…I am Ritesh. Ritesh Garg." I took out my hand.

She shook it and smiled.

"I guess we know each other…" she smiled.

"Oh that's great to hear." Shrey said.

I exchanged pleasantries with Ashish, Sanjay and Narayan and spoke for a few minutes while Tia and Shrey were out.

Once they were back, Shrey joyously exclaimed, "LET THE PARTY BEGIN!"

Bacardi, Scotch, Whisky and Rum…everything was made available from Shrey's dad's cellar. All in the room other than me got excited at the sight of it and started pouring them out like it was water.

Shrey forcibly put a glass of whisky in my hand and the smell was nauseating.

I felt like puking but I didn't. Sip by sip, I started taking in the drink and my mouth burnt. There was this horrible bitter and strong taste which was making me throw up but I still drank.

I finished my glass with a lot of difficulty but to my horror- Shrey refilled it. By the time, I finished my second…my so called friends were already done on their third and were high.

Ashish, Sanjay and Narayan were playing *ringa ringa roses.* While Shrey and Tia were getting cozy. Shrey rubbed his nose against her throat and bit her ears. Tia pulled him closer and kissed him on his chest. Shrey pounced on her unashamedly in front of his friends and started pawing at her top. And before we could realize they both were grappling each other, furiously kissing. They attacked each other with wet kisses and took turns to fall on top of each other. Things were getting hot in the room and it was evident by the way Ashish, Sanjay and Narayan had stopped their *ringa ringa* to watch the show.

Things would get out of control I thought – so still on a high, I shouted, "Time up you Crrra-zzy l-l-loovers!" I went closer and pulled them apart. Still trying to hold on to the sensation, Shrey licked his lips. Tia looked at him with seductive interests.

"Con-trroolll" I said.

Shrey laughed it off and managed his emotions.

"S-h-it down!" I shouted at the trio of Ashish, Sanjay and Narayan. "Lish-en!" I said again.

Once all of them were settled down..I observed each and every face.

They all looked at me in rapt attention. And then with tear filled over emotional eyes, I narrated them the insult Aarushi and I had to face in the hands of Laharry!"

After I finished with my story -all of a sudden Sanjay stood up in a burst of madness and screamed, "REVENGE!"

Ashish and Narayan joined in chorus, "REVENGE!" Tia and Shrey kissed each other and said something that sounded like *revenge.* So everybody wanted revenge but no one had the f**king balls to tell me what to do.

"I do." Ashish raised his hand.

"We will blow his balls." Narayan joined.

Shrey stood up. He was of short stature and fair. His curly hair was all askew and he picked a glass from the table and threw it on the floor with all his might, "Laharry…here we come!"

All six of us laughed and laughter echoed in the room. Our hooliganism continued for a few more hours before I was dropped back home at four in the morning. Luckily, Mom and dad had no clue that I was out of my room for so long.

I had sweet dreams of Aarushi and then another one of seeing Laharry blown apart by crackers. They were really nice and lasted till I woke up at 11AM the next day.

Revenge is Sweet

"Here's the plan," Ashish said as he laid down a map of the school corridors and classrooms.

"What the f…" "From where did you get this??!" Shrey asked dumbstruck.

"School office….they have one of the pipelines as well!" Ashish smirked.

I looked at the proceedings silently as I had no other option. I was not wholeheartedly supporting what they were about to do but again I had very little choices. It was I – in the first place under the effect of alcohol, who had conceitedly pronounced that *revenge* was required. And now, I was the only one who was getting yellow at the thought of Laharry getting *ball blued!*

Impatiently I moved closer towards the table to get a better view of the map and what I saw was truly mind boggling. This map was equivalent to the Marauder's Map used in Harry Potter. Name any corridor, office or room – this map showed everything.

"So what's the plan?" I said.

"Nothing much…" Ashish rolled up his sleeves.

Shrey looked at the map with keen interest while he completed Ashish, "Yea! Nothing much, Sanjay and Narayan will be patrolling the corridors near the Staff toilet on the third floor. While you Ritesh will be waiting somewhere close by…"

"My job is to wait inside the staff toilet and bolt it from inside. My job is the most dangerous and if things go as per planned – it'll be fun!" Ashish resumed.

"And my mission is to plant device Charlie…" Shrey finished.

"Wo! Hold on, hold on! I ain't getting head to toe of what you guys are bloody talking about?" I had been informed about the initial bit but this military language was simply passing over my head.

"Our plan is to lock Laharry inside the washroom and burst crackers that'll scare the shit out of him!" Ashish said excitedly.

"And if we get caught…we are out!" I said helplessly.

Ashish hurled a few abuses in his local dialect, "Now who has the guts to take on Ashish Singh? Remember…I was the one who lifted that mathematics teacher, that too with one hand…remember, it was my father who said that if I am not passed then he will burn down the school. Ashish Singh is not afraid of anyone."

"Calm down Ashish…I can understand your…" I tried to pacify.

"Understand what Ritesh bhai? I understand nothing other than your problem…and revenge!" He shouted.

I shrugged and continued to pay attention to their haphazard plan.

"Device Charlie is Constipation pills. It will allow Laharry to run his ass to the toilet. And that's where we nail him!" Shrey tried to make a point.

"Nice." I said.

"But how will Ashish escape?" I had second thoughts.

"He will wait till Laharry faints..." Shrey replied.

"And what if he doesn't?" I asked.

"Then, I will beat the shit out of him...*revenge!*" he landed his fist on the table and it shook ferociously.

I stood near the water cooler and watched the proceedings in silence. Narayan and Sanjay started patrolling the corridors – fifteen minutes before the mission was about to take place.

Shrey had planned decoys to distract any teacher from going towards the corridors. He had gathered about six to seven children from ninth grade who would start creating a racket at the other side of the corridor when given instructions. So any teacher other than Laharry who would come this way were bound to be diverted in the opposite direction.

I sincerely prayed that this plan worked.

Three minutes before the commencement of the mission – Ashish arrived and slipped into the toilet with a huge bag hung around his neck. The bag contained crackers.

In another few seconds, I saw Shrey hurrying towards me. Instead of coming towards me – he went past me and didn't return.

I was nervous; I didn't understand what it meant. I continued looking from behind the water cooler as sweat crept upon my forehead. My legs were shaking a bit out of anxiety and fear of the consequences.

But before I could think further – I could see Laharry and his big fat ass. He was running like a cheetah towards the toilet door. The constipation pills had amazing effects which were evident in his expression. The chemical reactions had a terrible effect on his large intestine and in a fraction of a second, he vanished inside.

And then, out of nowhere came Shrey. Running faster than Laharry, he bolted the door hoping that Ashish would do the same. Mission Revenge commenced.

Sanjay and Narayan increased their vigilance while Shrey and I stood near the door with bated breath. Five minutes had gone by and we heard nothing. And then eventually, there was the sound of flush and zipping up of pants. The attack would begin any moment ...tick tick...tick tick...

The clocked ticked away. No sound of the attack and it had been good five minutes since we heard Laharry zipping up.

"I guess they both are hooking each other." Shrey said.

"Shut up!" I snapped.

"I swear they are..."

I didn't reply. And then there was an enormous explosion from inside. It shook the entire floor. There was silence again.

After three more seconds there was another one...it was louder. And two more followed continuously. This led to a commotion in the classrooms close by as children started creating pandemonium.

The explosions didn't subside and what was really amazing was that each explosion was followed by Laharry's shrieks.

" B A M . . . . A A A A H ... B O O M . . . . A A A H . . . . B A M BAM....AAAH AAH...BOOM....ARRE!"

The shrieks were heard loud and clear.

Teachers were slowly stepping out of their classes to check what was happening. Not deliberating the issue further, I unlocked the door from outside. This would ensure that no one suspected any foul play. In another good thirty seconds or so – Shrey and I rushed to call a teacher and complain about this 'weird noise' we were hearing from the staff toilet.

Our script was thoroughly prepared and we were mentally ready. With concerned faces we told everything to the teacher that we could… 'Mr.Laharry went inside and started creating these noises'.

Teachers were least interested in our bull shit and were more interested in calling the curator of our zoo, the principal – Jacob Martin.

Believing in Martin's madness, we decided to take a hike from that place. Sanjay and Narayan followed suit and within moments of utter perplexity amongst the children and teachers: we merged with the crowd and were never ever caught.

Our only worry was Ashish. But a small tap on my shoulders eased all the stress, "Hi guys, finished your physics practicals?" Ashish stood there with a physics notebook and a studious smile on his face.

"What happened? What's the commotion all about?" He winked.

I winked back.

The news that reached us that day was that Laharry was found all *white* in a spot of bother. His face had the expression of seeing a ghost and mentally, he was disturbed to the hilt.

A few days later, we got to know that Amit Laharry from Saint blah blah blah…has put in his papers. To our bewilderment, Jacob had accepted them.

Amit Laharry was no longer a part of our zoo. Out went an animal!

Revenge was sweet….

"So revenge is sweet isn't it?" Ritesh asked proudly.

Saniya's eyeballs seemed to have popped out, "You did that? I mean you...actually did that?"

Ritesh smirked, "with a little bit of help from my friends...actually a lot."

"Yes and the best part of this entire plan was that no one got caught...never!" Pallu said.

"That is so damn amazing!" Saniya replied.

They sat in silence for a few minutes and stared at each other.

"Sooooo?" said Saniya.

"So what?" Ritesh asked.

"Continue...idiot..." She reframed her sentence, "I mean tell me what happened after that."

"Time flew by as exams neared and we were busy mugging up the lines of our text books. The profound difficulty of understanding the concepts and terms involved in the chapter called the Magnetic Effect of Electric Current and Trigonometry made our head reel. I tried making tables and notes on better...."

"STOOOOOP!" Saniya shrieked.

"What?" Ritesh said worriedly.

"I don't want to hear this nonsense! Tell me about Aarushi. What effect did that incident have on her?"

"What do you expect? She'll come running all the way to me...give me a tight hug and kiss me all over the face?"Ritesh was sarcastic as usual.

"Kuch toh hua hoga..."

"Nahin. zyada kuch nahin. Since Half yearlies were round the corner, she didn't get much time to think about this. And neither did we get much time to talk to each other."

Saniya looked in rapt attention.

"...we saw each other regularly at tuitions – but talks never crossed beyond a 'hi' or a 'hello'. It seemed boring at first and irritating when you actually are itching to talk to someone. But, later on I gave in to the thought that our main aim was to study there. And actually Orientation was no meeting point of lovers." Ritesh finished. He got up, adjusted his seat and sat down again.

"That's so boring....so is this how your love story ended?" She asked.

"Initially I had this very feeling...but a small incident changed what was supposed to be an ordinary ending." Ritesh's eyes sparkled.

"WHAT???!" Saniya jumped up.

"Half Yearlies...!"he replied.

"Oh!" she sighed.

"Half yearly marks to be precise....I got a percentage high in the eighties while Aarushi barely managed to pass. The only subject she did well was English and Social Sciences. Others were disastrous." His tone reflected melancholy.

"How come marks played such an important character?"

"You will get to know, very soon...but for that I would point out two things in order to enlighten you. Number one, this incident took place after the Half Yearly marks were out. And number two; we had another two months for the pre board examinations. The Pre Boards were the main criteria for securing your seat in the school and getting your selective stream before your board results are out. So...for a student, Pre Boards were as important as Boards."

"Now will you continue??!" Pallu spoke after a long time. He seemed impatient.

"Ok...ok...ok..."

A Visitor in the Dark

"So, there are two techniques of drawing a circle. *Widh* or *widhout* using the centre of the circle. I hope you all have your geometry box so that we can..." Gupta Sir instructed the twenty five students present in class.

"Ch-ch-ch-ch...charssiii...circle *banayga*?" Manas asked.

I turned a blind eye.

"Charsi, are you all prepared for your pre boards?" he added.

In the background, "...we draw perpendicular bisector on AQ and then placing the compass on M we draw a semi..."

"Uffo! Let me concentrate...!" I tried to shut him up.

"Concentrate on Bhooka Aam?"

"NO! Concentrate on drawing a circle..."

"Okay! Okay! Charsi....look...look." Manas pointed his finger towards Aarushi.

"What?" I couldn't stand staring at her for long, it made me feel uncomfortable. I felt this urge of rushing up to her and hugging her.

"She too is drawing circles…" Manas made roundish three dimensional figures in air.

I could afford a smile.

"Why do you love her so much?"

I was taken aback by the type of question.

"What sort of question is this? Why do I love her? How the hell would I know that answer?"

"But still…kuch toh reason hoga…" Manas lingered.

"Haan hai!" I said in disdain.

"Tell me!"

"Well, see…when you don't have reason to love anyone; that is exactly when you know that you love her or him. He's fat, he's dark or maybe he doesn't have any quality in him. She's horribly ugly but you still love her. Hmmm…when your friends ask you the reason – you keep on thinking. And this, my friend is *love.*" I explained as good as I could.

"So you say that you don't have any reason to be addicted?"

"Yes…and I realized that, the day we fell into shit trouble. Any guy would back out but somehow I managed to stick on." I looked at Manas briefly, he seemed lost. "Manas…are you listening?"

"Yes, yes…go on…"

"So yeah, as I was saying is that – whenever I tried to start afresh, I got this feeling of sticking on and on…and then when I tried to find out the reason of why I wanted to stick on – I never got anything." Manas looked on clueless. The background music continued, "We will learn how to draw tangents with given angles of inclination…"

"So what I mean is that...love is blind, love is deaf, love is mute...love is crazy but wait on – love is *love* when you don't have any reasons to fall for that person a million times...!" I continued.

"You want me to clap...charsi?" Manas snapped.

"No...obviously not. You were the one who wanted to know!"

"I didn't want a poem with four different words on one line. Unfortunately your poem had four different types of love on one line..." he took out his tongue.

"Whatever..."

"You want her back badly...don't you?" he asked.

"No, I don't and this question is rattling my nerves."

"*he he he...*" Manas had a nice laugh over it.

I chose to pay attention in class and not pay attention to his questions.

I stepped out of the stinking basement after the class got over.

There were two exit points and I chose to take the one, I seldom choose...the rear one. Manas had some work, so I was all on my own. I wanted a breather and what better than the rear side.

Casting one last glance at Aarushi, I turned around and walked towards the rear gate.

At times, surprises do please you but for me – it was not supposed to be. I had a terrible surprise waiting for me at the exit point where I was least expected. Call it my dreaded luck or anything else - I met the XY chromosome(d) Aarushi standing there with a grumpy expression. Aryan could piss in his pants or even tease a hundred women but a thing he could do with great difficulty was to flash a smile. He looked at me in great disgust and so did I. At school, we seldom spoke to each other…and deep within, I knew the volatility of this meeting.

"Yes, I do"

"What do you want?" I asked without even thinking what his reply could be.

"I am here standing on my own free will. This is Sector 34 and you don't live here. My sister studies here and so you don't have any business to ask me what do I want." He spoke like a robot.

"Take a hike; she's on the other side."

"So, you keep a close watch on my sister...!"

"Least interested kiddo...!" I acted rude.

"I am not here to settle our personal grudges...I am here for a purpose." He said softening his tone.

"What purpose?"

"It is very important...I lied to mom and I am here now. I don't like lying. It's the same with Aaru di. So respect the effort that is required in lying."

I felt like yawning.

Aryan was a male form of Aaru other than the fact that he was far fairer in complexion and was shorter. He wore a loose floral shirt and Bermudas. There was this stupid pair of spectacles atop his nose which made me puke. Nevertheless, I loved his sis...so I had to show love for him as well.

"Ok...Ok...I respect your feelings involved in lying!" I said in a hurry.

Unknowingly, I placed a hand on his shoulder. He withdrew immediately, raised a finger good enough to poke my eyes out and said, "DON'T EVER TOUCH ME!"

"Wo! Wo man! Chill! You need my help...not me!" I said irritated.

"Fine..." he said grumpily.

"Listen carefully and don't interrupt...if you do – I will slap you hard." He said.

"Ohkay! That was a really nice warning...go on, I am all ears." I tried to act funny, he paid me no attention at all.

He began,

"There was a huge argument in my house last evening between Di, Maa and Paa. It was about her half yearly marks and all started off with your mention. I don't know, how your name cropped up – but yes, it did. And things weren't good. My parents pounced on Di and started teasing her and bombarding her with uncomfortable questions. Di couldn't tolerate and she replied back. This sparked off another round of heated discussions. In the meanwhile, dad read the circular Di received about securing seats in our school. It said that if she wanted Science stream in eleventh standard...she would have to get around upper eighties in Mathematics and nineties in Science. Honestly speaking, right from the time you entered her life – you ruined it. Her marks fell like the twin towers. She is in such a state that she can't even concentrate and attempt to do better. You have ruined her! All my brothers: Samarth, Sarthak, Aarav, Abhinav, Mukut…are studying either engineering or medicines. All of them are my first cousins and are topper respectively. All had taken science as their stream in eleventh standard. Why doesn't my sister deserve this chance?? If she doesn't manage to do what Maa and Paa wishes – I know how they'll start behaving with her. And Di was crying last night and she told me that if something like that happened…it would be the worst thing possible. And sadly, she said that she had no hope…but I think she does…" he finished with tears in his eyes. With his throat all croaky, he looked up at me.

"I understand your plight brother…what do you want me to do…?" I felt helpless.

"Do you actually love her?" his question was direct and hard.

"And why do you ask that? You are just twelve – these complexities will perturb you." I tried to explain.

"Yes or No?" he barked.

It could be a trap I thought but immediately after that I said, "*Yes, I do.*"

"People mostly get irritated by you but there is something about you that attracts them…" he started off again.

"What do you want to say…speak clearly." I said impatiently.

"You seem to have a solution to every problem. Please help my sister out…make amends to the misery you have caused. I promise to you Ritesh bhaiyya that I will do whatever I can to ensure that she comes back to you…but please help her out."

I was taken aback. It was a Brett Lee bouncer that struck me hard.

I rubbed my eyes for a second.

"Aryan…!" I was about to say something when he interrupted.

"I have no idea whether Di likes you or not but I am sure that if you offer to help – she would accept it. Maybe seeing your effort, there'd be some change. Please do something."

"Tell me exactly what to do?"

"You are good in studies, pretty good – help her out in your own way and ensure that she gets into Science. Ensure that she is saved from her parents."

I stood silent, thinking about everything he spoke about. All made sense, since I had ruined Aarushi's life: it was also my responsibility to help her stand up again in a small way. All of a sudden, something cropped up, "Aryan…Aaru told me something about moving to Kolkata. If it is true, then why is she afraid about securing her seat…?"

"She lied. And I don't know the reason." He replied bluntly.

I nodded in approval.

"So will you help her out…?" he asked.

"*Yes.*" I said politely.

"Good. If you had said *no,* then I would have knocked your head off!" signature dialogue delivery from Aryan. "Chalk out a plan and I will meet you very soon to execute it…for now, thank you and good night." He winked at me and before I could realize anything, he was already walking towards Durga Housing Society. I didn't want to call him back as it would take me a million reasons to change my mind.

I had no specific plan as such on how I would help Aaru out in this busy schedule of boards. But, I knew that I would manage something…and more so – the present circumstances of Aaru, told me that I should stand by her.

If every word spoken was true and I did love her…it was time I showed it.

So I did…

Different Shades of Grey

*Jaane Kyun Dil Jaanta Hai…tu hai toh I'll be alright…*my 5130 Xpress Music started vibrating and singing at the same time.

An unknown number flashed on the screen…trusting the Vfone idiots, I decided to ignore the call. In brief moments of tranquility, I went back doing what I do the best – contemplate.

So, I thought. *What should I do?* I asked myself. On one hand – I had some cleaning up to do in my life. On the other, I had been assigned the task to help out the love of my life in God damned mathematics and science. I was stupid enough to accept the proposal (for the first time someone had proposed to me) from a jerk who I hated from the bottom of my heart.

Aryan was indeed the sole reason of getting caught last time around. If it wasn't for his constant licking business, I still would have had a blissful and flourishing love life. But what to do?? When you have a brother-in-law who is hell bent upon beating the shit out of you with his strange actions…can't help it can you? I found it bizarre that almost twenty four hours after I had accepted Aryan's request, I was having second thoughts. Well, the second thoughts weren't related to whether there was a lack of genuineness in my feelings towards Aaru but to the very fact that a seemingly complex procedure of communicating without getting your arse kicked had to be implemented. Confusing and incoherent? Let me explain; Radhika aunty and her husband had made my survival very difficult indeed. I was handed out a list of DON'T s before they could actually agree that they'll not spill a single bean to my parents. The list was somewhat like this:

1. Don't stalk.
2. Don't talk.
3. Don't visit our apartments.
4. Don't look at her.
5. Never ever call.
6. No letters.
7. No Hi and Hellos.
8. No birthday gifts.
9. No New Year Wishes.
10. No show of interest towards anything related to her.

This list, dated February 2009 was amazingly hilarious. Not neglecting the pissing off content it carried…I had a great laugh over it because the very next month, I landed up in the same tuitions as Aaru. As a result, this grave crime of mine resulted in another point being incorporated, "No looking here and there during class hours!"

In short, my life was being run by a fearsome lady, her idiotic son, her confused daughter and a bunch of friends who constantly reminded me of this deep infatuation, I had fallen to. For all of this I had a straight answer – *f**k you!*

I am in love….!

The phone rang again, sorry I'd rather say – Vishal Dadlani started shouting again…it was the bloody same number and I seemed to be in a very good mood to *break the* ….of the asshole who was constantly disturbing me. So, I received the call.

"Hullo!" I said exasperatedly.

"Is this bhaiyya?" that voice replied.

"Oh Hi…" I said in a prolonged murmur. It was Aryan who had called.

"When do you start work?" He sounded imposing.

"When you teach me, how to disobey those beautiful eleven rules handed out by your mom."

"You were born a disobedient child giving the nurses a lot of trouble, so in that case, it wouldn't be too difficult to disobey those rules would it?"

"Yeah why not…" "…just come to the point and stop shitting around."

"Mind you language!" he barked as usual.

"You mind what shit you are saying…." I said.

"Oh really? ….doesn 't seem nice when a piece of garbage talks big!" he countered.

"I am garbage…? Eh? You must be cow dung and a little bit of skin with a whole lotta flesh!"

"What do you mean?" he found that line to be a bit above his levels of comprehension.

"I mean that you are insane and a big idiot…who is blessed to have a sister like Aarushi. And now, if you don't know how to shut the f**k up – I am hanging up!"

"Hold on….if I hadn't loved my sister, I would never have tolerated you." He said.

"Yes, and if I have tolerated you – it is all because I love your sister." I mumbled inaudible sentences.

"What did you say?"

"I said that it is very difficult to make you understand that I don't have time for your nonsense."

"Really?"

"Yes, really… Trying to make you understand basic principles of life is like teaching Radhika aunty how to fall in love."

"Stop insulting my mom!" He scowled.

"I didn't insult your mom…I just said that she is a bit weak in this subject. I think your dad must have tried his best till now? Right?" I was bashing him up in words.

"Ok. Leave the topic."

I enjoyed some sadistic pleasure. That boy had huge amounts of attitude stuffed into his ass. But that attitude wasn't enough to bully me.

"Thank you for allowing your mind to realize that you were wasting my time." I said.

"When do you start work? Stop procrastinating and stop giving lame excuses."

"I'd love to start work any day, but what about your sis?"

"She agreed reluctantly when I told her that a pest was finally coming of use."

"Oh…and?" I was tired of fighting with that thick headed jerk.

"And, she asked me to devise a plan and so have I!"

"Great to hear…go on and tell me how your master plan is like!"

"Are you fit enough to climb walls?"

"What?"

"Are you deaf or are you in a mood to trouble me. I said that are you fit enough to climb walls?"

"Are you an idiot or do you think I am one? Am I some Spiderman? Or am I that Rahul of Kuch Kuch Hota Hai?"

"You are nothing. You have spoiled my sister's life and you will mend it." He snapped.

"Tell me sire….!"

"Every night, my dad returns at 10. We finish dinner by 10.30 and all go to sleep by eleven. Keeping half an hour for falling asleep, you have to reach our house at 11.30."

"That is *some* plan…in short you want me to be kicked by your parents and beaten by mine, right?"

"Wrong…you have to do this much."

"And how long do I stay?"

"Say…for two hours daily? Seems fine enough to guide my sister."

"Oh-kay!" I shuddered at the thought of two hours in Radhika aunty's den.

"I will keep the door open for you most of the time, if in case there is some problem – you have to climb up to the parapet."

"Oh-kay." I repeated.

"Deal is done?"

"Yes." I said.

"Good. Thank you bhaiyya." I could sense the joy in his voice.

"You are welcome *saala.*" I replied.

"HEY! You abused again! What the hell...."

"Shut Up! I meant brother-in-law!" I stopped his sentence midway.

"O"

"Thank god, good sense prevailed." I let out a sigh.

"No *saala waala* now. First you give me and my sister what we want, then..."

"Then?"

"Then I wouldn't mind calling you *jiju.*"

Oh heavenly father. You have been so gracious to me for this inch of space that'll allow me to enter Aaru's life again. Thank you. I spoke to the one sitting above. I believed that he was playing all his cards and I anxiously wanted to see how he would shape my story.

After disconnecting, I remembered something a friend had once told me; this world doesn't have people who are either black or white. All people are shades of grey including me. Some are darker shades while others are lighter ones. And Aryan was a lighter shade of grey – irrespective of his bitchy nature, there remained an adorable self in him and that made him as adorable and lovable as Aaru.

A Memory and Lots of Trigonometry

"Shh....not a sound!" Aaru pleaded.

"I know, I know, stop reminding me!" I curtly replied.

Aaru led me through a narrow passage within her flat. It was actually the balcony on the rear side of the house. It was hell dirty, but I avoided saying anything about it.

My wrist- watch read 11.40 P.M. The crickets buzzed in the background while Radhika aunty's snores gave them company. I tiptoed past their room and with a great deal of cautiousness, I entered Aaru's room. And that too, for the first time!

Her room was decently sized. It had a double bed, neatly arranged cupboard and a bookshelf containing Aryan's books. They had two bedrooms in their flat so with great difficulty she had to share it with Aryan.

Speaking of Aryan, there he was sitting on the bed with crossed legs and folded arms. He had a nice and short military cut with which he was looking quite good. He had got Aaru's smile and it suited him well. Before leaving for 34, I had promised myself that no matter – how bad Aryan behaved…I would not retaliate. And I was determined to ensure that it went off that way.

Once, I was in – Aryan dimmed the lights and shut the room door. He took a bean bag and stuck it to the door. Then he sat down on it, nullifying all the chances of getting less time to react – if in case, Radhika aunty made an appearance. Aryan's presence near the door would ensure that the slightest of sounds would be heard by his fox like ears.

"Can I sit?" I asked.

"Consider this to be your room other than my cupboard and its contents." She replied.

"Seriously, I am least interested in trying your amazingly sexy tops."

Aryan let out a coughing sound…indicating that he too was present and would keep a close eye on both of us.

Aaru smiled on seeing my reaction.

I settled down on the bed, she sat opposite to me.

"So, how did you come?" She asked.

"By flight – amazing experience!"

"No time for jokes…seriously *batao,* how did you come?"

"I cycled across. It wasn't too much of a hassle."

"And how did you leave your house?"

"My house is built for silent escapes. I created a mini set in my room. Stacked up all the pillows under the blanket and made it look like I am fast asleep. I then, climbed down the service stair case of the balcony – took out my cycle and left."

"Stupidity at its best. If I find that you are wasting too much of your time, I won't allow you to come again." She said.

"Stop loving me so much, will you?" I said without thinking much.

Aryan coughed again. I understood what it meant.

"So where do we start?" I said changing the topic as quick as possible.

"Trigonometry…I hate it." She made a sad face.

"Rule number 1, you won't get anything by hating a subject…just try falling in *love* with it."

Aryan's cough gave me a reminder that I was not here to discuss love.

"Okay and?" she inquired.

"And, by falling in love with it – you will understand what each sum wants you to understand about trigonometry. If you want to know trigo, then consider each sum to be a facet of its life. Love those sums and you will love trigo. And when you love someone, you want him badly don't you?"

Three quick coughs followed my sentence.

"Every action has a reason behind it and that will be understood later on. For starters, learn these sentences by heart: *Some People Have Curly Brown Hair To Paint Black.*"

"By any chance do I look like an amateur? And what the hell was this hair thing?"

"I am teaching you the basics so that your pro attitude doesn't fail you in an exam atmosphere. So will you shut up and listen?"

"OK Sir!" she giggled a bit.

"See, S stands for Sine, P stands for Perpendicular, H stands for Hypotenuse, C stands for Cosine, B stands for Base and T stands for Tangent."

She listened in rapt attention.

I continued, "In this way – we know the three basic trigonometric ratios by heart and by inversing them…we will get the other three." "Get me?"

"Yes sir." She nodded.

"Stop saying sir!"

"Ok sir…I mean Ok Stupid."

"So now what you do is to try and solve these selective questions which are expected the most." I handed out a sheet from my bag, it had about five or six selective questions.

"So you are starting from the basics are you? Giving me another sleeping lesson?"

"Look Aaru, I'm sure that Laharry shithead didn't teach anything…so let me give it a try? And you will get double practice when you visit Orientation tomorrow!" I said.

"Yeah yeah…Gupta is no less sick that Laharry, ok I will do these sums. Don't sit under my nose, it's distracting…so just check out stuff in my room other than my cupboard."

"I should be the one distracted…" I said.

Two short coughing noises followed from the direction of Aryan.

"HEY!" I barked at him.

"WHAT??!" he replied.

"Go get yourself some cough lozenges. You are pissing me off!"

"Go to the loo…" he said.

"Why shou……OUCH!" I couldn't complete what I was saying as Aaru was pinching me hard.

"WHAT?" I asked her.

"MOM WILL WAKE UP! So please speak softly!" she begged.

"Ok…ok…" I looked at the other side and started observing the books Aaru had.

Aryan stared at me as though I was some big diamond thief observing the 'Diamond Comics' in his cupboard.

"You like reading comics?" He asked from his 'guard house' (the door).

"Yes…love them!" I replied.

"Good…can I show you my collection?" he asked enthusiastically.

"ARYAN…don't trouble him!" Aaru looked up from her notebook and spoke.

"Arre nah nah! Its fine, you do your sums…let me pass time as well."

"As you wish," she shrugged and went back to her work.

Aryan jumped up to me, leaving the door bolted but unguarded. He took out huge compilations of TinTin, Asterix and Chacha Chaudhary. He started narrating a small story behind every comic he showed me and it made me nostalgic as well.

Seeing Aryan so enthusiastic about his past, I was pushed down memory lane. It was a time when life was simple and things weren't so complicated. I seldom had to think for myself with so many people to pamper me around.

My *mama* was in his college days and did part time jobs. As a result, his earning was not that great. But, he was regular with his promises which included one movie a month and whole lotta ice creams and comic books. So I remember him getting me those Batman comics which I would die for every week on Friday. His 10 o' clock walks also interested me a great deal and I used to join him most of the times. My *mama* was that inspiration for me to grow into what I was today. He often gave me experiences rather than lectures. His small pranks and jokes generally had loads to say and if there was any person with whom I felt secure after my dad…it was my *mama.* I knew very well that, *mama* loved me a lot so I also knew that it gave him all the authority over me. And I seldom crossed the boundaries he set for me.

"Ritesh bhaiyya?" Aryan spoke my name sweetly.

Childhood memories had made me emotional and I remembered that it had been over two weeks since I last spoke to *mama.* My desire to make my future normal hindered in the way of my normal past.

"Yes tell me." I replied softly.

"Liked my comic collection?"

"Loved it." I unknowingly stroked his hair as Aarushi watched in awe.

"What happened Ritesh? Is everything alright?" She asked looking at the sight of the century. It was a half truce between two bitter enemies.

"Yeah yeah. What about you? Battled through the sums?" I asked.

"Yes, check them."

"Wait I'm coming. In the meanwhile, Aryan – please go back to your guard house." I pointed towards the door.

"Here it is." Aaru handed me her copy.

I checked the sums diligently as I had already done them twice before coming, for my own practice sake.

I went through the sums and understood each mistake with great interest. In all the places where she managed well – I put a smiley and a comment. In places where she went wrong, I pointed the correct way.

After checking the lot, I gave her five more sums to do and then taught her a new topic from trigonometry.

By the time, it was 1.30 or so…I couldn't keep my eyelids open anymore. I asked her to stop doing those sums.

"That is enough for today." I said.

"Ok."

"So I leave now and I will see you again tomorrow."

"Will be waiting for you," she managed a faint and tired giggle.

I looked towards the door; Aryan had fallen asleep on the bean bag. Both Aaru and I looked at Aryan for a while and then turned towards each other. As our gaze met – I felt that same old urge to say that I loved her. But somehow, I restrained. We looked at each other for few more moments as she slowly lowered her eyeballs. My hand not listening to me crawled up to hers and placed itself upon hers. She didn't react for a while and I felt she gave permission to whatever was happening or was about to happen. I felt the warmth generated in my body and didn't want to let go off her. Gathering up courage, I spoke, "Please come back…"

"Please come back tomorrow or else…" she mumbled the same words.

"Or else what?" I had her hand in mine; I expected something like 'I will die without you'.

"…or else, I will fail in Maths. You are indeed an amazing teacher Ritesh *sir!*" she mocked my emotions for a while.

I yawned, "Yeah yeah…will always come back for you."

"If you don't leave my hand and go, how do you plan to come back?" She asked, pointing towards our clutched hands.

"Oh! Sorry!" I withdrew immediately in a bit of embarrassment.

"So are we meeting tomorrow?"

"I guess we are – if you aren't going on a date," I was in my sarcastic best.

"Not really….never had that practice you know." She winked.

I smirked; it was indeed the right time for me to leave.

Habits those are Bad

Bad habits are always considered bad. On second thoughts, how silly of me to say such shit! Pardon me. *Ahem ahem…*

So, why did I raise the discussion of bad habits all of a sudden?

Oh yes, Gupta and his bad habits were getting on to my nerves – so, all of a sudden during the mind raking class of Chemistry…I felt this urge to stand up and slap him hard. But, I couldn't. He wasn't that bad I thought.

Gupta strolled around the class, irritating every student he crossed – girl or boy he could tease anyone with his lame jokes and dastard comments. Nevertheless, his quality of being a tremendously gifted teacher helped us ignore his dark spots. Other than teasing his pupils, Gupta loved repeating the phrase, *time please* …every ten minutes or so. According to him, he had a class exactly five minutes after ours got over at another tuition centre (located a kilometer away). So, as a result – he had to carry his heavy mass and run to that centre to attend his second class without being a nano second late.

His good habit of punctuality often led us through long hours of irritating... *time please* questions.

I generally sat on the third row from the front. Aaru sat on the fourth row and Manas shuffled places between me and another guy from his school. Most of the time, Manas acquired a seat next to me but since the last few days, he was always being blessed with the front seat. The front 'blessed' seat was the one which received the most *time please* bombardments. Manas was obviously pissed, his face clearly indicated that. Five straight days of *time please* was like a wart on his ass. Knowing Manas well enough, I knew that he would surely come out with something drastic.

So it was.

It was a usual class, brimming with boring jokes and stupid comments. The occasional *time please* did crop up and Manas was as usual bearing the brunt of it. Strangely, Manas' attire didn't seem that appealing that day. Normally, he dressed trendily with the latest fashion but today, he was covering his T shirt tightly with a torn and dirty denim jacket.

Gupta strolled past him, occasionally passing him a comment or two regarding his mowgli hair and dangerously sarcastic smile. Manas chose not to react and Gupta took that to be his submissiveness. Little did Gupta know that Manas had a plan B for him. In fact, even I couldn't have guessed what the plan was...till it was eventually executed.

Gupta had finished three rounds of *time please* and was about to commence the fourth or the last round. We had just ten minutes of madness left for the day and would be in the open air again. In those ten minutes, one expected Gupta to repeat his favourite phrase at least once if not twice.

The signs were ominous; he cleared his throat and walked past the first row. He reached the third row and scratched his fat nose. He looked around at the students and walked back to the front row. He cleared his throat again and played with his fingers for a while. For the first time, the students got a feeling that they would be given respite from his last round of phrasing around. In all good spirits, we were about to let out a huge sigh of relief in unison just when he cleared his throat emphatically. And exactly like a car before it starts…we understood what the throat clearing meant. It meant that we wouldn't be saved from the final round like we had imagined initially. Two short coughs and then came his awesome dialogue delivery…with perfect precision and knowledge of nuances, acting the most natural one can be…Gupta said those words, "*Time please.*"

The two words were an atom bomb. They fell and exploded or maybe exploded even before falling because Manas' reaction was surely explosive in all senses. He jumped up from his chair, still clutching his jacket closely to his chest; he leapt up in the air once or twice. He circled Gupta like a wild monkey and gesticulated that he was about to tear his hair apart with one hand. He stamped his foot on the ground and showed his anger by clenching his fists. Gupta stood there dumbstruck, completely taken aback by this apelike behavior from the mowgli of his class. Momentarily, he forgot that it was about time that he should dismiss the class. He forgot that he was the teacher of the class who had to maintain discipline…he forgot that the boy displaying rude antics against him was younger than his son. What Gupta could only judge was that Manas was completely sick of his *time please* business and wanted respite from it. Manas' madness was justified. As the high pitch laughter of twenty five died down what followed was another round of euphoria for them. Taking a short break from his antics, Manas stared at Gupta with venomous looks.

"You and your *time please* has pissed the hell out of me!" he shouted at Gupta.

"What say you?" Gupta mumbled.

"I say that just *shut up*." Manas retaliated.

"I…." Gupta was about to say something.

"Time please, time please, time please….for ten days, I have had enough time to please you into not eating our small brains like this. For your *time please* and your eccentric self, I have something to show."

At this point of time more than ninety percent of the students i.e more than twenty two of them thought that Manas would do the drastic act of showing his third finger. Which incidentally he didn't do. Instead, he just let go off the denim jacket and as it slipped down his chest, we saw something glittering. It was a 1950s material made time piece which had a decently big clock hung onto a metallic chain. As the time piece moved from left to right – still attached to Manas' neck; Manas brought out his chest and withdrew his abdomen drastically. It gave the impression that he was offering people to take away his rights of virginity. He showed off the time piece with puffed up chest and ensured that he had the last say, "This time piece is for you, you moron. At least students will be saved from this terrorism that you have started…and before you can start terrorizing me with your threats of throwing me out, I want to point a small thing out."

"Wha...?" Gupta's abnormally big mouth was in short of words.

"I quit!" Manas slammed the time piece on the floor and stormed out of the class.

The students couldn't decide whether to cry or to laugh. So, we all decided to laugh till we cried out of pain in our stomachs.

A Battle to Fight

"Now that was rude!" Aaru scowled.

"What was rude?" I asked surprisingly.

"You know...laughing away at the sight of Gupta being insulted!"

"Ha ha...but definitely kudos to a certain Manas, who relieved us from *time please*!"

"Not a good job done, at all!" She started walking at a brisk pace.

"Hey! Listen up..." I said as I walked faster to catch up.

We had just left the basement and the repetitive statement of the freshness of air outside must have become boring by now. So, to add a little bit of newness – I'd say that after so many months, Aarushi had actually allowed me to trail her. *Progress, Master Garg*, I said to myself.

"...did you understand what all I taught you in Trigo last day?" I finished my sentence.

"Oh yes." She paused. "I surely did." She said.

I gave her that *no more sarcasm* look. She understood immediately.

"No sarcasm…I promise!" She said.

I smiled as I trailed her all along.

"So, what's the plan?" I asked out of stupidity.

"*Dobara se* plans! I am tired of them now! What do you expect? A date with you?" She replied irritated.

"*Arre nah nah! Aisi kismat kaha*?" I had given up hopes of a date. "I was talking about the next class you'd want." I lied.

"O! Sorry for exploding. Actually, I hate people pestering me." She tried hard to smile.

I nodded my head in approval.

Her apartments were just round the corner when she slowed down (something usual and most expected). She stopped and turned to look at me.

"See, thank you for all that you are doing for me Ritesh. But…but don't you think erm this might be a bit too much, eh?"

"What will be a *bit too much*?" I mocked her.

"You know, these classes you are taking – the nights that you are staying awake, etcetera…etcetera."

"If this is the main bone of contention, then I must tell you that I love the prospect of getting to share my knowledge…the little I have! And, when it comes to staying awake…haven't I done that before?"

She felt embarrassed and I wanted to kick myself immediately.

"Not exactly that, but…but…erm…hmmm….well, you know…*chalo* leave it!" She wanted to say a million words but ended up saying only five or six.

"As you wish." I shrugged.

We stood briefly unnoticed by the crowd and untouched by time. We seldom found ourselves in situations where we ran out of topics rather to find ourselves discussing more than two things at one go seemed quite pleasing.

"So?" she asked after the brief pause.

"So what?"

"Are you coming tonight?" she queried.

"Do you want me to?"

"Yes obviously…" she had said a word too much. She rectified this mistake instantly, "As in, it'd be great help if you did." She flashed a heart melting smile.

"At your service at eleven thirty ma'am!" I bowed.

She smiled again and I smiled back.

A few more nano seconds till she was gone. That big black void reappeared…a few more minutes was all I needed, but never got. Life was hard.

It got harder when I reached home.

"Ritesh, I need to speak to you." This was the first thing dad said the moment I entered.

"For what?!" I snapped like usual.

"It's important son." Mom added.

"Coming…" I said totally pissed.

I barged into their room.

"Tell me." I demanded.

Mom kept silent as dad started speaking, "It is been over three months now and I felt that you shouldn't be kept away from all of this."

He looked at me for a reaction. I was a complete zombie.

He continued, "There was a massive raid in my office a few months back. And something happened that I had worst feared."

"What?" I asked.

"My boss was caught in a web of loopholes in illegitimacy of his bank balances." He said.

"So?"

"So, as a result, after further investigations – he has pleaded guilty and faces imprisonment."

"And?"

"And, today – the company has fired as many as seventeen employees and unfortunately the list includes me as well." His expression was that of nonchalance. He was calm and composed as though he was void of feelings of a mortal.

The last few words fell like bomb shells. "WHAT!??!" I asked.

"With effect from today, I am no longer employed. All my funds have been cleared. I am what you call, jobless." He was perspiring.

I didn't reply.

Mom who till now was a silent spectator, joined in, "There is a slight incorporation of changes in our life from today onwards."

"What?" I asked.

"Your dad and I are going to challenge this decision. So we have got a lawyer in Delhi who is helping us out. The case demands that we stay in Delhi for a week or so, but we can't afford to disrupt your pre board preparations…"

"I will come with you where ever you go!" I interrupted big time.

"…tch tch, listen dear."Mom shut me up.

"WHAT?"

"We want you to stay here and look after the house. You are a big boy now, I guess there wouldn't be any problems?"

"No, there wouldn't." I lied.

"Just as I expected."

"But this isn't fair! I mean, you guys can't just keep me out of this. As in, c'mon – aren't I supposed to be a part of this family? This battle is mine as well."

"It is yours my dear. It is. But the difference is that you will fight this battle from inside. You will ensure that nothing goes wrong when we are away."

I nodded.

"…you will promise to be a responsible young man and take care of yourself and your studies, your food, clothing, etc. All finances will be provided; you have to be responsible enough." Mom finished what she had to say.

"Honestly, tell me how long will you be away? It doesn't seem a week to me!" I said angrily.

"It maybe two or three or even more." Dad pointed out despite mild protests from my mother.

I was at the verge of breakdown. So here I was, all alone…facing another battle in the game called life. Securing marks, winning back your girl and now a new agenda, *take care of yourself.* I had no idea on how to execute this seemingly impossible task. The thought of being away from Mom and Dad sent shudders.

"I will manage," I tried my best to not let them down.

"We knew you would." Mom got up and move towards the door of the room.

"So what now?" I asked her.

"A little bit of organising left. We will move to Delhi tonight itself."

"Don't go, please." I wanted to say but all I did say was, "All the best!"

Amazingly, for the umpteenth number of time in my life – I found myself between a rocky place and the high seas.

The Return of the Minister

Sleep keeps away the hungry stomach. And that was exactly what I was trying to do. I was trying to sleep in class while Narayan was trying his hand at a relatively tough algorithm that wasn't even taught at school and Sanjay was making pictures of nude girls.

"10th *toh pass kar le,*" Sanjay directed a statement at him.

I was no more than a silent audience to whatever they were talking about.

"Why do you limit knowledge to class?" Narayan seemed unperturbed by Sanjay's sarcasm.

"Because I study to pass the class and not gather knowledge like apples…"

"Yeah, you are right. But I think that it is the other way round," Narayan said in between inserting values into the algorithm.

"Other way round?" Sanjay asked.

Narayan nodded.

The Battle and the War

A week later…

"Ritesh, what's wrong?" Aaru nudged me.

"Nothing," I said avoiding her gaze.

"No, something must be wrong…just tell me!" She demanded.

"Said nah, nothing!"

"Just shut up and TELL ME!" she hissed.

I looked up at her. The moment our eyes met, unable to lie anymore – I started crying.

"Ritesh bhaiyya?" Aryan who was guarding the door, rushed towards me.

Tears were rolling down and I made futile attempts to control them.

"What happened dear? Please tell me." Aaru was stroking my shoulder.

"Told you nah…NOTHING! Just practicing being emotional."

I let out a short laugh.

"Bhaiyya *batao na*! Did anyone say anything to you? I will break his bones. Tell me, tell me, tell me na!" Aryan pleaded.

"Aryan, GET LOST!" Aarushi shooed him away. After which she said, "Ritesh, please share this with me. I promise to give you a solution. Crying away will only pile on your miseries."

My tears had stopped. I wiped the remaining traces from my face and held myself together.

"It's very difficult. I can't," I said outright.

"Okay! Don't tell me the difficult parts…tell me the easy ones – just the way you help me in mathematics." She held onto my shoulder, something I was enjoying.

"Aaru, if you leave my shoulder – only then can I sit up properly," I said.

"Ha ha…sorry *stupid*," She let go off my shoulder immediately. "Now tell!" She said.

"Fine. It is something like this…" I said. "…my father was working in this packaging firm for donkey's years. He had this tremendously gifted working staff under him and a wonderful boss. But, it all changed when his boss was caught in some illegitimate funds in his bank account. That's when all the problems started, you get me?"

Aaru nodded.

I continued, "So, the income tax people penetrated deep into the boss's account and hell of a lot of black money was found. And the very next day…under some bloody IPC, dad's boss was arrested. There was this amazing hue and cry in the company when everyone started running for cover here and there. There was complete madness in dad's office and the higher authorities went to any extent to save the reputation of the company. And…"

"And?" She asked.

I took in a deep breath, "…and started firing many people. My dad was one of them. He was convicted to have been a part of the boss's illegal funds."

"WHAT?!" Aaru exclaimed.

"Yes, exactly what you heard. My dad was fired overnight. So, it left us with a weak bank balance, an emotionally volatile family and a cause to fight for. My mom wouldn't let go off this social and financial injustice done. So she challenged the decision."

"But how can you possibly fight a company?"

"That's what I felt and I still feel now. Of all that I could gather, our savings are being drained out in order to fight this case. Not a single fired employee is challenging the decision other than my dad. They bloody, seemed to have accepted whatever has happened. Hence, this is leaving all the cleaning work for us to do."

"Wow! Such things happen only in films," she said.

"Films are a spiced up version of our lives," I said.

I got up and started strolling in her room, "Mom and dad have been away for a week or so. They are in Delhi, lodged in some disgusting guest house. The lawyer is hopeless and my dad is financially unstable. I can't light a freaking gas burner let alone make food. I have been attending school in rags, my neighbours are big snobs, my exams are near and I am missing my parents. Can anyone deserve some punishment like this?" I asked her watery eyed.

"No, I don't think so," She said.

"And this is exactly, what is happening to me! For God's sake, I have not touched food for a day or two!" I cried out.

"WHAT!" Aryan and Aaru leapt up in unison.

"What the hell are you saying?" Aaru asked.

"Yes, my life is hell. I guess, I will fail in my exams but the last thing I want to do is to keep my promise. So, till the pre boards – I will be coming everyday and would be urging you to do well. Scoring well is least you can do to lessen my miseries."

"Ritesh! This is unfair! You can't do so much…after all, I hate you! I HATE YOU STUPID! You have not been eating for TWO DAYS?! How can you be suicidal? You are coming here every night; can't you ask for anything dumbo?"

I could only smile seeing her concerned.

Aryan started hissing, "See bhaiyya, mom and dad are sleeping – so you better not make me shout! How could you do such a thing when we were around eh? Anyways, let's not deliberate this – from tomorrow onwards, I will smuggle food for you. You can have your dinner here. Fine?"

His sweetness touched my heart. "Fine," I said.

Aaru walked up to me, "Ritesh… I know that you have done some silly things and you have hurt me and many people around you. But, that doesn't mean you are a bad person. You are just the wrong guy at the wrong place. Understand?"

I nodded.

"So…" she began. "We will not give in to fate. Be strong and pray that your parents remain that way. They are fighting against injustice and as you say, it's not only films where miracles can happen. Okay?" She tried to comfort me.

"I guess. But haven't I wasted too much time today? What were we supposed to do?" I asked.

"Today we were supposed to revise Refraction of Light," she pointed out.

"Oh! It's Sad that we won't be able to complete it. Anyways, take out your notebook…I have an interesting observation."

"What?" she asked while taking out her notebook.

"You know while writing down the refractive index *1n2*,we are generally confused about the media we will use for giving respect to in the sentence…right?"

"Yeah."

"It's simple. Just consider the *n* to be a door and consider *1* and *2* to be walking in from right to left. Then, we can say that we show respect to a person and allow him or her to enter a room first. Same way here; Speed of light in 2nd media with respect to speed of light in 1st media is the refractive index." I smiled in a sense of brilliance.

"And what about writing it in numerals? Which comes on top?" she asked.

"Aaru, haven't you noticed already? I give Aryan too much of respect and look at what it has done…he has started sitting on my head. The same way giving media 1 respect allows it to sit on top of media 2 and hence, it becomes the numerator in this case."

"Wow! Nice observation." She chuckled. Aryan glared at me. I glared back.

When my parents were fighting a battle – I was slowly winning a war. *The war of reunion!*

La-Harry

"Liked it?" Aaru asked.

"Oh yes, it was hell tasty…who made it?" I asked back.

"Mummy did. This is Aryan's favourite dish."

"Nice nice," I said licking my fingers and cleaning off the delicious *matar paneer,* Radhika aunty had made that day.

"Do you want more?"

"No…it's fine. We ought to be studying now." I didn't oblige.

Mom and dad were still stuck up in Delhi. I hadn't seen them for a long long time and my life was getting miserable by the minute. Luckily, I had someone like Aarushi by my side who was slowly and steadily transforming into a friend, a good one. Advice, guidance and help – name it all, she was there to shower on me. I was grateful to God, that a time had come when we would be close again and surely this tough situation helped me get closer to her. I avoided missing classes, unless and until it was dead urgent – I didn't find any reason to miss. There were two reasons behind this and the main one was that I had fathomed the pangs of separation and was now quite aware on how it felt to have the one you love the most close to you. In fact, very close to you.

By routine, Aryan had been smuggling food for me for the past few days. Radhika aunty may have been merciless to me but her food was delicious. And, if I ever had to congratulate her for something other than giving birth to her daughter, then, it would definitely be for the food she cooked. *Delicious!*

Being all alone helped in escaping from the house unnoticed but on the other hand, it increased my responsibilities as I had to ensure that every door was locked and every window was bolted before I could leave. Just in case of a burglary in my house, I'd be short of excuses, I thought.

So, Aarushi was handling things quite well. Steady progress in Science and Maths had given me hopes of a brighter tomorrow. I saw a time in the near future when aunty would be sending her to my place for maths tuitions – however, when I contemplated deeper, I realized that this time would only come in the wildest dreams of mine.

"I have a problem," Aaru said softly.

"What?" I asked.

"I don't understand the chapter on triangles and circles It's hell difficult…look at these suggestive questions will you?" She pushed towards me a bundle of question papers given to us from the school.

I quickly scanned them for the third or the fourth time. "I agree…" I said.

"…they are indeed difficult. Many of them, I don't know myself."

"Haw! What will happen to me then?!" She gave the expression of being paranoid.

"Nothing will happen…just relax," I took in a deep breath to visualize the next course of action.

"Ritesh, we can't go to school can we? During the prep leave?"

"I guess not. But there must be some way that we can solve these." I asked myself.

"What about the ones that you are unsure of? I guess your guidance is good enough but don't you think you need some proper person to verify all that we are doing here?" she posed another problem.

"Yes. You are right," I said still thinking.

"Who do you think will help us?"

"I guess I know someone who would." I smiled.

"Who? Bhooka aam?"

"No, no! He is a no hoper. Someone with sheer brilliance and a little bit of madness," I said.

"Who stupid?"

"Laharry! Amit Laharry!" I exclaimed.

It was a small drawing room with a smaller coffee table and an even smaller TV. Aaru and I shared glances nervously. There was the aroma of vanilla extract in the room which definitely made our visit worth it.

I tapped my feet impatiently as I waited for Laharry to arrive.

"Pssst! What do you think? Will he agree?" I hissed at Aaru.

"Dunno stupid," she giggled.

"I guess he will, if he doesn't know the culprit of the fire crackers incident."

She nodded.

In the meanwhile, a familiar voice beckoned our attention all of a sudden.

"Oh what a wonderful day and wonderful visitors," Laharry barged into the room taking both of us by surprise. We stood up to greet him but were in turn greeted by his Oxbridge accent, "Sit sit, my children. And what need does bring you here to the humble home of Amit Laharry from Saint…blah…blah…"

"Sir, actually – we had some work," Aaru said.

"Aaah…young Aarushi, is that correct?" he asked.

Aaru nodded. "Sir, we need your guidance for our pre boards," Aaru said.

"Why only me? I was kicked out of the zoo wasn't I?" he chuckled.

I flashed a sarcastic smile, "Not really sir…we miss you!"

Laharry sneered on hearing that, "You LIE!" he said.

"…no one ever wanted me there and no one is either missing me. Don't lie to Laharry!" Laharry jumped up from his seat and paced the floors of his room.

"Sir, but I did!" Aarushi pointed out.

"I know I know but haven't I been harsh to you once or twice?" Laharry asked.

"Yes sir, but teachers are like our parents aren't they? How can we retaliate?"

"Yes, yes…you make sense – but still…why is master Garg lying about the importance of my presence?"

"He isn't lying sir…he is just trying to tell you that things aren't bad as you feel."

Laharry stopped and sat back on his reclining chair.

"What do you want me to do," he asked with a straight face.

"Give us some study material and tell us how to go about things." I said.

"Then what happens to those brilliant coaching classes that you join?" He behaved like a maniac.

"Tuitions are meant to be for wastage of money…" Aaru began.

"Then why do you go there in the first place?" He stopped her short.

"…well, we go there to…" Aaru wanted to clarify but I felt that it wasn't the right place to clarify things.

"Can we have this debate later on?" I intervened.

"Sure sure…tell her, not me." Laharry sneezed.

"Are you helping us?" I asked point blank.

"Hmm…." "…let me think, I might…so what do I get in return?"

"…you get our love and respect," Aarushi made herself clear.

"Oho! Love and respect…strong words my dear, use them well."

"We do sir…most of the times," I said in an assuring tone.

"Ha ha…I feel so young again," Laharry chuckled.

"You do?" Aaru said removing a strand of hair that fell on her eyes.

"Yes yes…fine, I will be your friend, philosopher and guide," Laharry said.

"Wow! That's nice to hear, thank you," I faked.

"Thank your stars my friend that I have so much of free time. Laharry is always searched by jobs but nowadays Laharry searches jobs. Ho ho ho!" he acted as though he delivered a Filmfare speech.

"…*thanda ya garam?*"Laharry asked indicating on whether we wanted cold drinks or tea.

"*Filhaal* nothing!" I said courteously.

"So, Master Garg – how should I be of help to you?" He cleared his throat.

"Nothing much…you just keep us up to dated on whatever is going on in the world of mathematics. You know…common errors, silly mistakes, type question, etc. Just let us know whatever you can. That'll be all."I said.

"Not a problem!" Laharry replied.

"So, this means that we have your side. Is that so sir?" Aaru asked.

"Yes, young girl – for sure!"

"That's all we required. It's getting late, I guess we should move." I got up to leave. Seeing me, Aaru did the same.

"Aaah…as you wish," Laharry got up to leave us till the door. "…and yes," he said.

"…do forgive me for my rudeness in class would you?" he looked at Aaru when he said this.

I knew that Aaru would rather die than be in a situation when someone is asking more than a *yes* or *no.*

"Obviously yes sir," she replied.

Laharry smiled, "Off you go then…" he clapped his hands in old British style and pointed towards the open door.

We bade him goodbye and left. Now, I had an official mentor.

Siddiqui

"*Namaste,* are you Ritesh Garg?" the peon asked.

"*Ji,*" I replied.

"Come come...*saab* is waiting for you."

I followed the short statured guy into a room where he looked as though he was a citizen of Lilliput. Even I looked the same...withholding my behavior of complaining against claustrophobic places, I got this strong feeling that God had made my room seem claustrophobic in comparison to the one I was standing in.

A huge archway led me into the main visiting area of the room, where the desired person actually met his visitors. The rest of the room which was theoretically termed to be for entertaining guests was a mini golf course. At one far end, I could see a huge shelf filled with books fatter than the thighs of sumo wrestlers. At the other end, I could see a liquor cabinet with imported brands of various kinds. There was a billiards table and a satellite radio set right next to the visiting place. Two huge revolving chairs made of leather dyed beige was kept for people like me to sit. While, there was an even bigger black one meant for the exclusive use of the person I came to meet.

His display board was filled with various quotes and law annexures. I was impressed, hell impressed.

He sat there impeccably dressed in a white shirt, black trousers and a black blazer. He played with the miniature Ferrari on his table while he spoke on the phone.

Mr. Siddiqui was a Law expert with expertise in company law. He had been in practice for the last two decades and had minted money with the help of his tremendous success rate in the wildest of wild cases. Siddiqui was Shrey's father and unlike, his son…he had grown up the hard way spending hours in studying under huge financial stress. I admired him for he was a self made man. I was familiar with his outlook at home but had never imagined that he had an office like this.

Nevertheless, I sat down and waited till he completed the call.

"Hi Ritzy!" he said.

"Uncle…now don't call me that," I replied.

"Why why? Your friends call you by that, don't they?"
"Yes, they do but still it's very girlish…avoid that will you?"

"Ok ok bubah. Master Garg, tell me…" he put his mobile phone on silent mode.

"See, it is a long story and something that is as important as my life. It will take time to tell, you sure you will help me out?"

"I will try my best to do so," he politely pointed out.

"No try…Shrey has been such a good friend of mine for so long. You have to give me your word that you will do it."

He looked at me with a vacant expression, "Can't fight with you can I? Okay, I WILL do it."

"Good. Then listen..." I narrated him the entire story with brief pauses in between. To make it more dramatic, I included the sub headers and footers that my dad used when he told me the story. I then told uncle every bad thing that has happened with us as a result of the incident. He heard me out with rapt attention. I could see that at times his phone was blinking but not once did he look at it; such was his commitment to every case presented to him.

After twenty minutes of mournful narration and after deliberation on every single detail that I had collected and reiterated, I indefinitely paused. Uncle was studying his fingers with extraordinary concentration. I didn't understand what it meant but I trusted it to be some sign of recollection or reorganization of thoughts reeling in his mind. After brief moments spent in observing fingers, uncle looked up to me.

"See, of what I see in this entire case...it seems that your dad got a raw deal," he said.

I let out a sigh of relief.

He took in some air and spoke again, "They just wanted a scapegoat and your dad fit the bill quite well. Who was looking after the case?"

"Some Sushil Yadav..." I said.

"Oh that's crap news. He is as corrupt as your dad's boss was. But..."

"But what uncle?"

"But, what I don't realize is that, how can I possibly put up a case in which your dad can sue the company for compensation."

"There must be some way..." I asked and said at the same time.

"There might be sonny, but at times things are not as simple as they seem or vice versa."

"What do you mean?"

"I mean, one never knows how many more loopholes will come out of this. Verbally, I can go with the fact that your dad is clean but to prove it will be a different case altogether. There will be counter arguments and false proofs. A company as big as your dad's will cross every pile of shit to ensure that their name is not tarnished. That's where my role comes into play."

I nodded as I didn't know what would be the ideal thing to say then.

"Can you ask your dad to meet me here?"

"Sure," I said.

"Ask him to meet me as soon as possible and you promise me something."

"What?"

"Today onwards, I am taking charge of this case. Your mom and dad don't have to stay in Delhi anymore and both of them can come back. But, in no ways will you get involved in this, in no ways will you discuss about this."

I nodded again.

"Even if someone raises the topic, you will avoid it. You will let go off all inquisitiveness about this case's outcome. I say so because you are too young to understand these things fully. Pre boards and boards are an arm away and you can't take the emotional toll right now. You understand?"

"Yes," I said meekly.

"I will give my heart and soul to ensure that your dad comes out clean. You give your heart and soul for your boards. Promise?"

"Promise," I said.

"Good, now show me a big smile and go back home. Study well and keep in touch with Shrey," he completed.

"Wow! Most impressive," Saniya said.

"Yes, indeed," Ritesh replied.

Pallu nodded in affirmative sense.

"So did he manage the case well?"Saniya asked.

"He did a fantastic job!"

"Really? How?"

"My dad received a phone call one fine morning. It was a call from his office, they had decided to withdraw all charges even before the final hearing," Ritesh said proudly.

"Siddiqui rocked!" Saniya exclaimed.

"Sure he did. It was his clout that had done the trick. He secretly leaked out the message that he had prepared a strong counter case or a defamation case against the company for maligning the name of a dedicated worker. Going by Siddiqui's reputation, the company didn't take a chance. They withdrew the case and avoided the chance of compensating for the harassment. They took my dad back and also put him at a higher rank. So obviously, those days of emotional torment had borne fruits."

"Yes yes...and I guess it had other effects as well, right? I mean due to this turmoil, Aaru got closer to you didn't she?"

"Yes, she did. At first she was very lukewarm towards me but seeing me stressed, she did all she could to ensure that I got all the comfort I required. Even Aryan chipped in at times."

Pallu ordered some fresh lime. Being a silent part of this conversation, he didn't have much to do or say.

"By the way, even Laharry had redeemed his image in my eyes. He started behaving like a perfect gentleman." Ritesh said.

"Really? Tell me more," Saniya was her usual self.

"Well, he would pass me those tips daily which in turn would

help me in clarifying all of Aaru's doubts. So the double coincidence of wants did wonders for us."

Saniya's eyes glittered, "So would it be correct to say that your normal life was normal again? He he…"

"Yes, it would. Gradually Aaru and I weren't feeling uncomfortable in each other's presence. At times, when we had time in hand before or after tuitions…we went for little teacher-pupil walks."

"Teacher-pupil walks? Didn't get you!" Saniya said.

"It was more of revision of formulas and discussion of concepts. It worked wonders before we had Orientation Assignments. It helped in securing better marks."

"It did?"

"Yes. There was this nearby park which would be the point of meeting. Aaru had become more mature than she was and those major issues of people seeing us had now become minor ones, but still existed in her. She was more or less comfortable as long as our topics were confined within studies. In case of external topics like our past relation…she used to start getting restless. As a result, I avoided those."

"Poor Aaru. Can you tell me any one incident of importance when you guys went for the walks?"

"Oh yes, I can surely tell two .First one includes the first time I got a little bit of hint from Aaru that things can be brighter in the near future. And the next one, you'd love to hear as it includes Pallu's first crush!"

Hearing this, Pallu scowled. He was hell afraid of annoying Saniya as he loved her a bit too much.

"I am dying to hear that…go on Ritesh, tell me both the incidents and whatever happened further. Pleaase!" Saniya begged.

"Chill, chill…I will. Just relax and listen, it is interesting." Ritesh changed his posture and resumed his narration.

Matter of the Heart

"*Paaji,* it's a matter of the heart...can you please step on the gas?" I asked the skinny sardar who was in charge of my transport for that day.

"Oh tussi fikar na karo..." his pumped up confidence did a whole lot of good.

I jumped into his auto and sped off on what would turn out to be a seemingly important journey in my not so important life.

We sped past the Noida traffic, breaking every signal and becoming victim of abuses ranging from mother to sister. We woke up sleepy Policemen and shook up *sans* civic sense pedestrians.

I was racing against time; Aaru had fixed up a meeting at 5.30. It was 5.27 and I was a good kilometer or two away from my destination. I wished that I had wings then I could have flown, I wished I was Harry Potter then I could have used the Nimbus 2000 and I wished I was not Ritesh Garg then, because I hated to see Miss Punctual annoyed!

"Lo ji thirty four aa gaya!" sardarji joyously stated.

"Thank you *paaji* ...keep the change!" I said, stuffing the fifty rupee note in his hand.

I glanced at my watch, it was 5.32. Aaru was supposedly free during this time in the evening when her mother went neighbourhood hopping; so it meant that she would not at all be late. And, it also meant that I would be in for a scolding for my not so punctual behaviour.

God help me, God help me...I am not late...she will not be angry, I kept on muttering under breath.

I quickened my steps and crossed a few apartments before reaching the meeting point – a hanuman ji temple. The temple, small but neatly organized was pink in colour. I was yet to enter that place even once and get a glimpse of *Bajrang bali.* Quite opposite to me, Aaru was quite religious when it came to visiting the temple every Tuesday. Today was supposed to be one such Tuesday; the only difference was that I too was invited for a visit.

Now, where is she? I muttered again. I quickly glanced at my watch, it was 5.35. I feared that she had left. I was standing in front of the temple afraid to go in and search for her. I felt that Hanuman ji would feel that I was in search of my love and he had no value in my life. All in all, I had no intentions of offending him.

I looked around nervously, trying to locate a familiar face, a familiar pair of eyes or maybe a familiar dimple cheeked smile. Although, chances of her smiling were less – I still hoped that I could get a glimpse of it...*I love your smile Aaru, 'cause every time you smile – you actually mean it,* I spoke to an imaginary Aarushi.

So what do I have to do? I asked myself. The evident and

immediate answer was to go inside, but still I had this fear of pissing off Hanuman ji which restricted me from setting foot into that holy place. Then, there was another question that popped up – *who is more important? Aaru or Bhagwan?*

"Aaru, obviously," the voice said from behind.

I turned around almost immediately to see Aarushi standing there with this familiar looking expression, raised eyebrows and a courteous smile and the pleasant part of our sudden meeting was that after so many days, our eyes met. And it was a happy moment for me at least if not for her.

"How did you know what I was thinking?" I asked surprised.

"Magic maybe," she shrugged her shoulders as I walked up to her.

"You are late!" she stated.

"I know, I know…sorry," I tried being as sweet as possible.

"At times, sorrys don't work! I have been waiting here since 5.20."

"Not my fault…you said to meet at 5.30 and now it is…"

"5.40!" she scowled.

"Exactly…just ten minutes off schedule and you reprimand me for that?" I complained.

"Ten minutes can change the world…!"

"Ok…" Void of all other options, I simply nodded.

"Follow me," she said and started walking towards the park next to the mandir.

"But what about Hanuman ji? No visit to him today?"

"No, he knows the reason of coming to the temple today…it was to meet you, so I better not give him false promises."

I shrugged my shoulders on hearing her honesty. Like most girls,

Aaru, began by leading the way but soon ended up being led by me. Being quicker than she was and oblivious to my heart's needs of initiating a conversation, I walked ahead in brisker pace. The only time I realized that I was ahead of her was when I stopped to tie my shoelaces. I turned around to see Aaru trying hard to catch up.

"DO YOU HAVE ANY IDEA WHERE WE ARE SUPPOSED TO GO??!" She shouted.

"NO," I said.

"Then why DON'T you take the trouble of WAITING!" in came the reply.

I stopped on my tracks and waited for fifteen to twenty seconds.

"Thank you so very much for actually stopping," she said.

"Anytime. So what's the plan?" I asked.

"Just reach a decent place where we can talk without being noticed by people."

"What's so secretive about our meeting??" I asked.

"I guess…we aren't supposed to meet are we?" she asked and said at the same time.

"Yes we aren't but why are we meeting in the first place?"

"Because I need to speak about something," she started leading me again.

This time I deliberately walked slower. "What do you need to talk about?"

"I need to discuss the life of the cry baby I know," she smiled innocently.

The smile turned me into ice cream, "Oh really? Ha ha…and who is that cry baby?"

"You stupid…!"

As if I didn't know that, I told myself. "Wow! Really?" I asked instead.

After walking for a few more minutes, we came to the corner most entry to the park.

"This is it," she stopped still panting.

"Nice nice…!" I said.

"How are you and how is everything at home?" she inquired.

"Just the way I was and just the way it was," I smiled back.

"So no more issues regarding your dad's job and all?"

"Nopes, not at all."

"I am really happy for you….!"

"What about you,, anything new?" I sat down next to her.

"Not really…today is my cousin's birthday – so will be attending the party shortly. I thought of meeting you before that."

"Oh yeah! You told me, today is ninth of December….erm….ninth…" I suddenly got reminded of something.

"What happened?" she asked seeing the sudden change of expression.

"You know what date it is today?" I asked her back in a serious tone.

"Yes, I do! You said nah…it is the ninth of December!"

"And what is so special about that, Aaru?"

"Dunno….but…..hey….wait…..lemme think…what's special about today…hmm…."

"You don't know right?"

"…..I guess not. What's it?"

"One year back, today was the day everything virtually ended," sadness crept in to my tone.

"What do you mean?" she seemed surprised.

"Our relationship; it ended on this very date last year, as in virtually speaking. Aunty got to know about my phone call this very day. How I wish things could have been different."

All the facial muscles of hers contracted and what it did was that it brought about a serious looking Aarushi in front of me, "It was meant to end." She said turning her face away.

"Look this side," I wanted her to stop avoiding my gaze.

"What??!" She turned towards me irritated.

"Don't you think that things should have been better?" I asked politely.

"NO! We had broken all the limits and that is the reason things couldn't have been better. And please let's not talk about this."

"But why? Why do we always turn a blind eye towards something that is so important yet so painful? Why?"

"Because there isn't an answer to some problems, Ritesh!"

"There is. I know there is, the answer lies within us. Just that we have to find it," I tried making sense.

"We could have only found it if things were under control…we lost focus!"

"What focus are you talking about? Grades? Love of parents? Or friendship? Which one? We lost everything, didn't we…? What did we gain then?" I sent a battalion of questions.

"We gained PEACE OF MIND!" she cried.

"No, we didn't! At least, I didn't. I still miss you…" I later thought that I had spoken a word too much.

"As if I don't……?" understanding the consequences of what she said, she immediately got up after uttering those blessed words.

"Sorry, I said a bit too much. Don't think about it," she spoke in a reassured tone.

"I won't. But can't things be alright?" I asked.

"Not unless…my marks change. You understand?"

"Yes I do," I could afford a smile.

"I think I should leave now, we have been here for nearly fifteen minutes now," she was ready to leave.

"Why did we meet in the first place?"

"At times we have reasons to say goodbye but do we have reasons good enough to meet?" she put forward her philosophy.

"I have no clue whatsoever," I shook my head in a state of cluelessness.

She smirked understanding my misery, "I felt like meeting you. Or you can say that I was missing you…so we met. If you think it was too much of a hassle then I am really sorry."

"No no no…which jack ass said that it's hassle…always a pleasure meeting you ma'am," I tried to assure her that I enjoyed her company that evening (which I actually did).

"Might be that I meet you again, but next time it will be with mathematics worksheets. Ok?"

"Not a problem….!" I exclaimed.

"Good," she turned around and was about to start walking towards her place.

"Hey!" I stopped her after she had moved a few paces. She turned back to look at me.

"...a last wave of goodbye would be sweet wouldn't it?" I asked. She didn't reply and stared at me surprised.

"And yeah...next time we meet...can I get you a rose?" I asked in sheer simplicity added to my previous stupidity.

She gave the biggest smile and the sweetest smile a girl could ever give. "Yes," she said and resumed her walk towards her house.

A New Entrant

I guess there was a proverb that said something like *old guard replaces the new* or *maybe new guard replaces the old* – so was the case in our school; a new mathematics 'teacher' cum principal had arrived in the form of Mary Jacob.

We were not supposed to be attending school, but crisp circulars ensured that we had to. It was made compulsory to attend the first assembly of the new lunatic who had arrived to torture the juniors and bully the seniors. The teachers were apprehensive of what material she would turn out to be and so were my friends who had now made a small huddle and were having a group discussion on that pathetic looking creature standing on stage.

A short cough like sound was enough to break their huddle. All eyes now shifted towards the stage and the ceremony going on – which was a cause of disruption in our preparatory leave or free *ka* holiday!

The sound was emitted from the larynx of an element named

Jacob Martin. He stood there grinning at all of us with his curly hair falling on top of his eyes, every time the wind blew.

All schools had delayed the timings but ours didn't. It was the coldest winter ever to be witnessed by North India and seemingly had no effect on the bunch of South Indians running our school.

"Good morning children…" Martin stretched his words.

"Goooood mornniiing siiiir!" was the reply from the students.

"So, classes one, two, three, four, five…..eleven and twelve; all are present here?" He started counting the classes present and ended up naming the school without the nursery block.

There was an affirmative reply in unison. Hearing that, pleased with himself, Martin tried to smile. And we hated when he did that.

"As you know children, I have become old…" he continued.

Thank God, you understood that, I said to myself.

"…so it means that I am a little too senile to run this great institution – you see," he completed.

No we don't, I cried out within.

The monologue on stage continued, "This means that a new principal has to be brought in and what better to have someone from my very own family….ha ha!"

What?! I said. *As if you weren't enough of a burden ass hole,* I mouthed.

Martin now started doing strange gimmicks with his hand imitating a B Grade football star arousing the atmosphere around him, "Ladies and Gentlemen, boys and girls…please welcome our new principal and new mathematics Head of the Dept. Incidentally, she is also the mother of my daughter…Mary Jacob!"

Saying this, he started clapping the loudest as children around me and him and everywhere let out what sounded half a boo and a very bad moan.

That 'wardrobe malfunctioned' lady fortunate to have initials MJ approached the stage. The way she walked gave us an impression that she was counting the steps to the mikes. She flashed a fake smile – *so like Martin,* I thought. That smile was horrible. The plaque on her teeth was visible and it sparked off a response which did not go down well with her. She had expected us to love her plaque, but our honest reaction made her shut her mouth. She smiled this time with her lips shut, she still seemed horrible.

"Ah…erm…eh…ah…uh…." She began speaking. According to sources, this was her introductory speech.

"…hullo children?" it seemed more of a question and reply was lacking in enthusiasm.

She continued with stop –comma arrangements, "Ah…erm…as you know…uh….I am Jacob Mary…uff…sorry, Mary Jacob or MJ as they say…he he …ah…I can't dance like him. Can I?"

Of course you can't! I wanted to shout.

"I am here to extend a hand of cooperation….uh….ahem….and support and solidarity and comfort….and…uh….erm…." she got stuck again.

Most unimpressive, I thought.

"I am you new principal and we will have a nice time, right?" she adjusted her dirty sari and caught hold of her falling spectacles.

She spoke in this horrible vernacular accent of hers which sounded worse than Basu's Bengali one. Were we born to go through vernacular extremists?

After each sentence completed, there was a huge round of applause. Perhaps that was the motivation for her to continue with her nonsense.

Honestly, she knows shit about anything. Pleased her husband into this, I cursed all inside.

"When…I was a kid…my teacher….blah blah….." she started off with something as 'beautiful' as the chronicles of Narnia.

There she goes again, I completed with this thought in my body when someone pinched me hard from behind.

I turned around to take a quick glance, it was Pallu.

"*Kya hai*?" I asked.

"I am in *love.*" He replied.

"With whom?"

"That girl standing over there," he pointed towards one corner of the stage where a pretty girl dressed in pink stood.

"Who's that?" I asked.

"Ex-princi and present princi's product!" Pallu exclaimed.

"W-t-f?" I barked softly as MJ f*cked our brains!

"Uff! She is their daughter….!" Pallu hissed.

My jaws dropped for a second, I simply couldn't relate to the accident of birth and to the madness of 'free from chicken pox' Pallu.

"You will hit upon her???!" I wanted to shout but couldn't, so I hissed.

"Yes…I guess I love her," Pallu pinched me again.

The madness on stage was on in full throttle.

"Are you sure?" I asked.

"100 percent!"

"Ohkay…so what will you do?" I asked.

"Meet me in the evening today, sharp at 5. Will tell you then," Pallu whispered.

I cast a confused look at Pallu before diverting my attention to the stage again.

Some shit is better than others, I thought. And I thought right!

Cupid Strikes Back

"What's her name?" I asked.

Pallu sat directly across the table as we dug into the juicy mutton ribs. He seldom looked beyond the pieces of meat and only paused to drink some water. It was perhaps the fifth time, I was repeating the question and Pallu was all so evasive about it.

"Shreelekha," he replied and started digging again.

I made a terrible expression, "What *lekha?*"

"It is NOT what-lekha, it is Shreelekha!" Pallu surprisingly paused and snapped back.

"I know...I know. But it must take great presence of mind to come up with such a name when your parents ape the Western world," I countered.

Pallu didn't respond. He was busy eating.

"Are you listening???!" I shouted out much to the annoyance of the young couple holding hands under the table, sitting right next to ours.

"Yes yes…!" Pallu promptly replied.

"Soooo??? Why does she have a disgusting name?" I asked again.

Pallu gave a frosty glare. I shut up.

To make this chapter more informative, a small flash back would not be of much harm.

It was the last day before our Christmas break and a season of hope awaited us. On the other side of the break lied what we call the epitome of all disasters…the Pre Board Examinations! It was the beginning of the end of relaxation and procrastination; a time had come when it was required to have breakfast with Thales, eat our tiffin with Gandhi, share our lunch with Caesar, make the evening snack for Kabir and then finally dine out with Mendell. Such was the condition of our lot of bird brained but hugely talented (in other fields like abusing, watching porn, teasing girls, talking, etc) bunch of students!

Amidst the total chaos of catering to the needs of so many people inhabiting your brain, Pallu had the secret desire of getting an extra inhabitant in the form of Shreelekha Jacob (that is what you call religious integrity).

A couple of years elder to Pallu, Shreelekha was preparing for her twelfth boards from some school in New Delhi. Dark skinned but tremendously good looking, I assumed her to be the eye catcher of the streets. She was a photocopy of her mother *sans* disgusting smile and *sans* plaque teeth. She was pursuing medicals as her career and Pallu wanted to do engineering and this very fact made their match so more interesting.

That evening, Pallu had taken a detour from his guitar classes in Sector 62 to Shreelekha's flat nearby. Forgetting that there were two potential dangers existing in that flat in the form of Martin and his MJ wife – Pallu proudly strutted about the entire apartment as though it was his father-in-law's. Partially correct, this statement raised all the eye balls when he introduced himself to our new principal, Mary as a *khaas* friend of Shreelekha. Surprisingly, he was unaware of the fact that it was Shreelekha who had answered his call on the door and mistaking her to be Mary Jacob, Pallu blurted out all the greatest lies ever to be formulated on planet Earth. Shreelekha not blessed with Mary's peanut brains tackled Pallu very well and shunned all his queries. It was only after she had bade Pallu with so many unpleasantries & only after Pallu had stepped out of the society did he realize that it was Shreelekha whom he was talking to and not MJ. Keeping in tradition with all the blunders he has committed in his life, Pallu took an about turn and marched straight back into the Jacob household. And this time, it was our mother Mary who was waiting near the door to answer him.

"And what happened after that?" I asked Pallu who was dipping his palms into the *finger* bowl.

"The case of mistaken identities continued…" he said morosely.

"What are you saying…?" I queried.

"I mistook MJ to be Shreelekha…." Pallu burst into tears.

"And…?"

"And, I told MJ what all I felt for her!" Pallu was howling now.

"And…?"

"And, MJ kept on looking at me…adjusting her hair…"

"And…?" I desperately wanted Pallu to continue.

"And she smiled at me…that disgusting smile…..!" Pallu banged his head on the table.

After hours of irritation and sweaty palms, the couple sitting at the table adjacent to ours got up and stormed out. *They were here to hold hands and not eat,* I told myself.

"You saw that plaque didn't you?" I felt sorry for him.

Pallu nodded, "Yes, I did....!"

"So, what did she say?"

Pallu's expression horribly changed, it looked as though he was made to swallow a dead rat.

"This is the sad part..." he said. "...she showed me her ENGAGEMENT RING!"

I couldn't help in controlling my laughter as MJ's reaction was 'terrific'. But, I also could feel for Pallu.

"Nice..." I mumbled.

"Nice? Eh? Nice....??"

"Not nice....?" I asked him unsure of what to say.

"Obviously disastrous as Jacob then marched towards the door out of nowhere, wearing a *lungi.*" Pallu narrated.

"*Lungi*???!"

"Yes, *lungi* ! A pink colored one..."

I imagined Jacob in a *lungi* and it so made me puke, "Then, what happened?" I asked.

"He shut the door on my face and started shouting at his wife with some irakam-warakam!"

My eyeballs increased in size in knowing this.

Pallu took in a deep breath and released it, "Sadly, now the entire teaching faculty of our school knows that I have a crush on the principal's daughter. And they have come up with a threefold plan of teaching me a lesson….!"

"And what the f*ck is that?" I stood up concerned.

"Fail…fail and again fail! They will make sure, I fail." Pallu moaned.

"How are you so sure that the school staff knows about this? As in c'mon, it just happened today!" I tried to see sense.

"Intuition…intuition…the end is near and it is an intuition!"

"Shut the f*ck up will you?" I scolded. I continued, "There is no freakin' intuition and get that clear. If you love Shreelekha, you will get her. Everything's written!"

"Really?"

"Yes, really. I think the same for myself as well. So we needn't worry."

Pallu nodded in approval to what I said.

"I will try and handle this. I promise to you," I had no other option to pacify him.

Pallu looked apprehensive.

I held his hands and convinced him.

"Ohkay!" He said.

Now how the hell would I help him out? I asked myself in a profound state of perplexity.

S.O.S

Aryan sat there, gaping at me with his donkey like looks. I avoided his stare and looked at Aaru instead. Seeing me stressed out, she smiled. It was comforting enough. "What's wrong stupid?" She asked.

"Uh, nothing really…" I spoke out. "…it's just that your brother gets onto my nerves at times," I whispered the second half.

Aaru flashed her dimples; it made my heart beat faster again.

"Really?" she inquired.

"Yes…!" I exclaimed.

In the meanwhile, Aryan kept on gazing me like I was some big superstar.

"Dude, I know that I look like SRK, but that doesn't mean that you stare at me like that!" I snapped at him.

"Oh! Gimme a break…I will never ever stare at you. I was just concerned about the bleak looking future of my sister…!" He replied coolly.

"What do you mean?" I asked.

"Arre! I am just feeling sad for her… 'cause if you guys end up getting married….poor di!" he shrugged his shoulders badly and wiped imaginary tears.

"Marry?" I asked clueless. Honestly, I had never thought about it and thinking about it was making my ears go all red.

I looked at Aaru with a big question mark on my face. She understood that something had got wrong and all of a sudden shouted out, "ARYAN! How dare you talk trash??!"

She then threw a pillow at him which he evaded. He gave the naughtiest smile he could give and said, "Oooo…acting pricey are you? Should I tell Ritesh bhaiyya all that you say after he leaves…?"

"YOU DARE DO THAT YOU PIG…!" she shouted again, unaware that Radhika aunty and her husband might wake up.

In a fit of rage, Aaru picked up the soft ball lying next to her bed and chucked it at Aryan with all her strength. Unknowingly, while doing so, she hit the steel glass that was kept by her bedside.

'CLUNK CLUNK CLANK CLINK CLUNK CLANK CLANK CLANK!' it emitted an ear splitting noise as it fell on the marble flooring with a clash.

And then all of a sudden things got silent. Aryan and Aaru understood quite well, how nasty this situation can turn or could have turned. And in moments, they tried to make as many amends as they could. They looked at each other angrily while both flashed apologetic faces towards me. I couldn't help in responding to those similar pairs of eyes all telling me the same thing, that they were sorry.

All three of us stood our ground for a few minutes.

The clock ticked away till…we suddenly sensed heavy footsteps. They could be heard from a distance and they seemed very very familiar to me. A war cry was in the air…MiGs were bombing the place with potential nuclear bombs and approaching our door was a ferocious lioness, a protective mother and a strict aunty…my brain flashed the signal in red and there was a siren that went off. The message was clear and simple, 'RADHIKA AUNTY APPROACHES. RUN.'

"Radhika aunty approaches. Let me run." I hissed.

"No, you can't how can you?" Aaru hissed back.

I could hear mutterings from outside the door.

"P-l-eaaase Aaru! Please!" I folded my hands and begged.

The handle of the door turned. I saw flashes of green before falling on the floor with a thud. My head hurt as it hit the marble flooring on the other side of the bed. In a state of recklessness, Aaru had pushed me and had caught me in unawares. Unbalanced and vulnerable, I fell on my head and rolled to the other side of the bed within seconds. My head was reeling and I could see proxima centaurs all around me.

Radhika aunty had entered the room. I could recognize her slippers as it was the one she was wearing when I had touched her feet almost a year back. Her slippers and pedicured feet were the only things I could see from my position.

If one side of the bed was exposed to the door, then obviously the other side wasn't. So, I had no clue on whether this act of Aarushi was a fluke or not but it did work. As, I fell to the other side, hurting my head…I realized that I was hidden from the line of sight or the 'line of fire'. This made my job of saving my ass easier. From underneath the small openings of the bed…I could make observations such as the colour of Aunty's sandals and her pedicured feet. But, the best part of it was that Radhika aunty couldn't see a single bit of Ritesh Garg. I smiled in glee although trying my best to control my breathing.

"Please tell me what is going on?" Aunty asked.

"Nothing," Aryan and Aaru said in unison.

"Then why do I hear clamour in the middle of the night?" the voice asked.

"*Mumma,* Di was actually studying…" Aryan tried to convince that cross lady.

"Your school has asked you to throw glasses around while studying?" Aunty countered.

I was biting my nails, still hidden but hell scared.

"No….but they asked us to throw balls around!" Aarushi had a counter argument.

There was no reply from Aunty. Although I couldn't see her face, I very well imagined that she had made that '*are you trying to fool me?*' look.

"Actually, *woh kya hai na*, we need to verify the presence of friction in the air which acts on a moving body, deaccelerating it's speed to a certain extent. And the relative speed of the object and friction posed gives us…" Aarushi spoke of something that did not make any sense whatsoever and also wasn't there in the syllabus.

"Ok ok ok….I know I know," aunty said even though she didn't understand a word.

Phew, I said to myself.

"It's quite late. Go to sleep now, do these experiments later," she moved closer to Aaru.

I guess she stroked her head or something and then walked towards the door.

Before leaving she said, "Good night my little angels…"

Little angels? I'd rather say…the devil, the angel and God, I told myself. *Why God?* The little voice in me asked. *Because God is invisible isn't he? And so was I today.* I answered. The voice seemed content but before it disappeared it passed me a small message. *Save our souls,* it said.

I got up. My head still hurt.

"Enjoyed?" I asked Aaru.

"Yes," she replied, wiping beads of sweat from her forehead.

"What's there to enjoy?" Aryan asked.

"That's *sarcasm,* you idiot!" I fiercely said.

"Shhh….Ritesh….not a sound!" Aaru interrupted. "Aryan, go and block the door and do your usual stuff," she ordered.

"We were lucky today," I said.

"Yes, absolutely."

Aryan in the meanwhile took his normal position of being the watchdog. He blocked the door with a bean bag and fell asleep on it within minutes.

"At least we can be assured now that your mom has to pass through a huge mass before entering," I chuckled.

"Shut up!" Aaru looked at me angrily.

"I don't think I should come from tomorrow onwards…" I said.

"Why?"

"Because c'mon, don't you think this can prove to be fatal?"

"NO!" She replied curtly.

"What no?"

"You have to come at least till the pre boards are over!"

"That is insane..."

"No...it isn't! You have to," saying this, perhaps hurt to hear me refuse, Aaru turned to face the other side.

I went towards her and held her shoulders and turned her slightly so that she could face me.

"Ok *bubah*..." I said. "...will surely come whenever you ask me to...promise!" I added.

Aaru tried smiling a little but broke into wild laughter on seeing my silly expression.

"But..." I said.

"But what?" she asked.

"But, you need to help me out in something..."

"Sure. Go ahead," her tone was comforting.

"Pallvinder has fallen in love with Shreelekha, the product of the principals!" I spoke as Aaru's expressions changed drastically.

"So, you need to help me out to help him in understanding the emotions of a girl who is two years elder to him. Ok?"

"Ok, but is he serious?" she asked the same question.

"Unfortunately, he is. And he doesn't know what shit he is landing himself into..."

"I agree. But we can't blame him. Falling in love is not such a bad thing at all," she replied.

My eyes glittered on hearing this, "You really think so?" I asked excitedly.

"I feel so…but don't start having your high hopes. You are miles away from getting me back," she smiled mischievously and exactly getting a feel of my pulse.

"How mean….!" I faked misery in my voice even though it was quite genuinely present.

"Like can't we be together again? Never?" I asked.

"We could have but you know, last time…" she started off again.

"…*we crossed all the limits!* I know, I know," I completed her. I partially aped her as well.

"*Jab jaante ho, toh poochte kyu ho?*" she asked.

"Because, I am so incomplete without you," I begged.

"Your Mathematics marks will be incomplete if you distract yourself like this," she pointed out.

"No, it won't. I promise," I was convincing.

She fell silent as my heart beats increased. When a girl becomes silent, it either means she's thinking about what you just said or she's making answers to shut you up or even both.

"Time is not right…" she spoke calmly.

"Ok. Then what about tomorrow?" I asked.

"Arre, it is not about today or tomorrow. It is in general, time isn't right for distractions sweetie."

I made a grumpy expression, "Fine! I am not talking to you."

"*Uffo!* You took it wrongly. Try to understand what I say."

"How can I?? Do you ever understand my emotions or what I have to say?"

"It's nothing like that..." she started off explaining herself again.

I cut her short, "No...no...no! Why is it always this way? Eh?"

"Okay...give me some time to think over it," she requested.

"How much time?"

"Say, till the boards are over?"

I wanted to crib over the long duration but immediately after that, I thought that something was better than nothing. Aarushi asking for time meant that I was making small inroads in to her life again.

"Fine," I said grumpily.

"That's really sweet of you," she smiled.

I smiled back and like usual started talking to myself, *angel's heart has been barricaded which I have failed to break through. Now, the only option is to take a few steps back and run in to hit it with greater force. Maybe that barricade will break or maybe it won't. But I will keep trying.*

"I will keep trying..." I said.

"What?" she asked surprised.

"Nothing," I shrugged my shoulders and stared into space.

Over Rated

"Two days remain," Aarushi folded her arms and tried looking angry.

I sipped in some Cola. We were standing in front of a roadside cold drinks stall in Sector 34. I had pestered and pleaded, I had begged and requested and finally Aarushi approved of meeting at such a precarious place where her so called *tons of family friends and relatives* could come to get a glimpse of this new age Romeo and Juliet. The latter part of the previous sentence was conceived by me and I never had the guts to tell Aaru about it. Nevertheless, Aaru's lame excuses of getting spotted everywhere irritated me like anything. I just couldn't explain it to her that we were not officially dating each other. But no, she had this reply every time I pointed out something or the other, *"Ritesh, I have been living here for fourteen years. Even the streets know me!"* And how would I reply? I would just say, *"No, no problem Aaru. You know, I have never forced you and I am no one to force you…"* And by completing that sentence, I would continue the tradition set by my predecessors of never ever disagreeing with a girl even if she wasn't your official girlfriend. I loved Aaru and as my friends complained, I was blinded by that love. I could never see any reason to justify my feelings but ended up seeing an entire Himalayan range consisting of reasons to justify every feeling of hers. Like for example, I just couldn't digest the fact that Aaru had this fear of being spotted by people who had so much to do in life. Take for example; her aunt who lived close by was one of the most feared. And why was it so? It was because she was a mini FM radio and would blabber continuously all day and if by chance she had seen us…it would mean coffins for Ritesh Garg who died while loving and loved while dying. But, c'mon the very fact that she would be busy in her circle of jobless people satisfied the condition that she wouldn't spot us. But my angel; my miracle never ever saw sense.

Remembering such instances irritates me. So, bunk it…

"So what?" I replied to her lame question.

"So what? Ritesh do you have any idea what our first exam is?" she got equally pissed off.

"Nopes," I replied.

"It is SOCIAL SCIENCES!!" she exclaimed.

"So?"

"So, we ought to be studying!"

"Okay, let's go to your place and study together," I said coolly.

"Hello?? It is *5.30 PM* not *AM*. Even if it was the latter, I wouldn't have allowed you to enter, huh!"

"Nice nice…" I sipped in some more cola.

She kicked me, "You listening?"

I nodded.

"Then, let's go back rather than waiting for that stupid friend of yours…" she urged.

"No way, don't expect me to that and don't expect me to allow you to go. We *have* to meet Pallu by hook or by crook," I said.

"Grrr….I feel like strangling you at times," she pressed the neck of an imaginary Ritesh Garg .

"Go ahead."

"I will *fail* in mathematics if I strangle you. So, I need to keep you alive till the boards are over…" she shifted weight on her feet while speaking.

I had this urge to complete her sentence, "…yes, you will kill me after the boards because that exactly is the time when I will ask you out again."

"No, I didn't mean that," she was expressionless on hearing me.

"Nice, nice…" I said and finished the remaining traces of Cola.

"Get away with your nonsense, that's the only thing, bad about you," she pointed out.

I shrugged, "want to have something? Aren't you thirsty?"

"Yes, I want to but I'm out of cash. You have any?" she asked.

"Yes," I cleared the last traces of notes in my pocket. "Here take it," I placed the notes on my palm and extended my right hand.

Her hand touched mine when she was about to take the notes and things blacked out for me. Her soft and gentle touch was majestic. It lasted a few nano seconds as Aaru fastened her action seeing my reaction.

She went away to get something for herself as I stood there gaping at her (with all pure intentions).

My phone rang.

"Hullo?" the voice asked.

"Hi Pallu!" I replied.

"Arre, where are you dude?"

"Here near the cold drinks *waale* uncle," I said.

"Ok…ok…wait m coming," the voice replied.

"Bye," I said and disconnected the line.

Aaru had returned.

"*Kya hua?*" she asked.

"Nothing. Pallu called, he is coming," I replied smiling.

"Ohkay, good to know that he is coming then I can…" she started off.

I interrupted her midway, "No, no…you aren't going back are you? You said you will wait. You are not going right?"

"*Nahi* stupid!" this phrase and that too coming from her sent jingles down my spine.

I loved being called *stupid.* And the only person who held copyright of that word was my angel.

"Then?" I protested.

"I was thinking of returning you your worksheets from my house after Pallu leaves," she said.

"Are you sure, I can visit your house?" I asked.

"Yes you can. Provided you wait for me at a considerable distance away," she set the terms.

I nodded.

"Good," her dimples shown.

"Oye Ritu!" a voice beckoned.

Aaru and I turned our faces towards its source. Towards us came a panting hippo in the form of Pallvinder Pandey.

With an addition of five kilos since I last saw him; his fitness levels over the years had taken a dip. I remember quite vividly, how he had climbed onto my verandah last year on an auspicious day when he had come to meet me. And now, asking this Pallu to climb up to verandahs would be like asking Yuvraj Singh to field at point and catch as brilliantly as he used to.

"Sorry *yaar*, got stuck at the park entrance…so I am a bit late," he apologized first up.

"Park entrance?" Aaru asked.

"Yea, the park of our apartments," he spoke directly to Aaru. "…it has this winding gate which we need to cross. So an equally fat man was entering the park and I was leaving it. So, the meeting of giants didn't help a bit as we took entire five minutes to maneuver ourselves out," he laughed at his own misery.

I afforded a smile as Aarushi chuckled.

"*Bol,* what help did you require?"

"Arre…it's the Shreelekha shit…" he said.

"You mean S square right? He he he…" I tried being comic.

Aaru suggested that I rather not do something I am terribly bad at, "Stop your lame comments please."

I raised my hands in surrender as Pallu spoke after the brief interruption.

"I spoke to her today," he said. "Actually, we met at the Christmas choir function last week and that was exactly where I noted down her number. And surprisingly, she didn't have any problem in giving me the number."

"Nice nice…" I said. Aarushi kept silent.

"So, I called her today afternoon and spoke to her for good fifteen minutes…"

"You call fifteen minutes *good?*" Aaru and I shared glances and looked at opposite directions almost immediately. We had spoken for five hours…once upon a time.

"No. Not at all, by your standards. But by mine, yes," he said with conviction.

"Continue," Aaru directed.

"While speaking, I deliberately raised last day's incident but she somehow didn't want to talk about it…"

"Come to the point, did you speak your heart or not?" I got impatient.

"Yes yes…I did," Pallu said.

"What did you tell her?" Aaru asked him.

"I told her that she was my life and I'd want to spend the rest of it with her," he smiled. "I also told her that I really really really liked her very very very much…!"

"And why did you use such personification?"I asked.

"It was to imply that I *love* her."

"So, you could have said that!" I shouted.

"Why the hell is *love* such a tabooed word?" Aaru followed up.

"Forgive me, but it is because of people like you…" Pallu pointed out.

This open insult or speaking of the fact pissed Aaru to the core and she no longer was a part of our conversation. She just twisted her lips and looked at Pallu angrily before going into a shell. For the rest of the conversation, she didn't say a word. I just couldn't help and care less.

"So, then what happened?" I asked ignoring Aaru for a minute.

"You won't believe what she said?" Pallu exclaimed.

"What??" I was excited; Aaru's eyes twitched a little as though she was trying hard not to follow the proceedings.

"She said that we can be together!" he leapt up in the air.

"WOW! That is amazing!!" I clasped my mouth in awe. Pallu had found a girl for himself. Exactly a few months back, I'd have sold my underpants to a stranger for telling me something of this magnitude but it did make sense now. Pallu was a man!

"But...but...but...." Pallu spoke.

"What?" I asked.

"She said that we needed to have *sex* to know each other well..." he added.

"What??!" I cried out. Even Aaru's jaw dropped hearing this.

"Yes..." Pallu smiled.

"How can you smile??!" I snapped at him. I was from a very conservative family and so was Aaru. We had still not understood about the right approach to sex.

"This is wrong..." Aaru said.

"What's wrong in *sex*?" Pallu asked.

"Everything. You are simply not mature enough for this. And that too with the Principal's daughter, you have any idea what shit you are landing yourself into?" She screamed at him.

Pallu raised his hands up in cluelessness.

"This can't be," I said. "Just stop this relation at once, if she wants sex then she doesn't want you," I completed.

"But what's the harm?"

"What's the benefit?" Aaru asked, dead serious.

"Dunno!" Pallu said.

"Then, please don't think about it...." I said.

"Hello?! You need to tell me about it...!" Pallu caught my shoulder.

"No, we won't. FIND IT OUT YOURSELF! Go and SPEND the night with her...!" Aarushi had got into a foul mood.

Pallu stood there trying to react.

"You simply have lost your soul," I said. "Pre boards are round the corner and you are interested about *sex*?"

Pallu opened his mouth but was shut up by Aaru, "Ritesh, please let's go from here. This guy is *sick*."

Aarushi caught hold of my hand and started walking away from that place, she dragged me quite some distance away and that was when I finally realized that she didn't want me to be in Pallu's company. Not liking the feeling of being dragged, I started walking along side her on my own free will. But, desperate to shun me from Pallu's philosophies, Aarushi continued to drag me along, holding my hands. This possessiveness towards what I am exposed to made me love Aarushi even more. While she dragged me towards her apartments and beyond, oblivious to our initial belief of people looking at us...I felt that Aarushi was correct in her judgment. *Sex* was a highly overrated thing for today's teen. At a time, when greener pastures awaited us, something as hyped as *sex* would destroy our ambitions.

I felt proud that day, because I was never attracted to Aaru physically. It was her qualities as a person, which attracted me and I loved her for that. And I was also blessed that Aaru too had never been with me for the mere intent of having *sex* like so many teenagers wanted these days.

It was indeed a sad day for someone like me who believed in 'love@15'; because all of a sudden it started having this physical aspect to it...

Penultimate Madness

I flipped through the pages of my History book in lightening speed. *Three chapters still to go, God...give me some more time!* I kicked myself for not working hard from before.

I went through the timeline of the evolution of novels. I hated that chapter even though I called myself a writer. Chandu Menon and Jane Austen were no wonder great men and women but the very thought of having to memorize each of their novel's name seemed too big a task for me. *Table, table...where's the table?* I asked myself. I scavenged for the table which I had made to make my job of studying this horrible chapter easier. My search was tireless and futile and reaped no benefits other than time waste. It was so, because the table I was searching for was actually stuffed up within the pages of my book and I had wasted almost half an hour before good sense prevailed.

Once I located the table, I misplaced the index to the map of Vietnam. So another fifteen minutes sped away in search of that. Once the map was found, notes of another chapter had vanished. As

I Am Not the Only One

I walked up the stone steps of my school and rushed towards my classroom on the third floor. It was a chilly morning and the gushing air was capable of making almost anyone ill. I avoided over exposure of my over sensitive body to the harsh weather and instead, entered my well heated class room.

Generally we leave our houses, appearing to be confident and well versed with whatever we have studied. This attitude in turn gives our parents high hopes and they start thinking that their children will win the world and come back after the exam. Much against the expectations, the child performs badly and goes on to blame the examiner for it. And so begins the teacher-parent confrontation saga which continues for ages. So, much to the contrary belief of our parents' perceptions, the children in my class were demonstrating that looks can be deceptive. They indeed were because not a single student other than Mr. Shaleen Lama was sitting down quietly, going through his or her work or doing the last moment revision. It looked as though, all the years' studying was to be completed in those two hours and it was bloody amazing to see that I was not singled out. I wanted to enjoy the moment and catch up with all the gossips going around and find out exactly who had studied and how much. I strutted along to my desk and then stuffed my text books under the table. I arranged my uniform properly and then walked along from desk to desk and student to student, to take their personal point of views.

I forgot that I still had three chapters to study...

I first went to Ashish, "Ashish *bhai,* all ready for your exam?"

He looked at me for a few seconds as those three earrings shone brightly. He hadn't shaved that day and had recently got a piercing done on his eyebrow as well. He had this amazing tattoo hidden underneath his rolled up sleeve. He got up to greet me, "Arre, *exam ki toh maa c*** di humne!*"

I didn't understand what he meant by abusing the mother of examinations so I kept quiet and smiled at him. I then moved on to the next desk.

Mr.Lama was sitting, "*Aiyyo* Ritesh! Havyu istudied??" he asked me in between adjusting his falling frames.

"Aiyyo, Mr.Lama! I havya nott istudied!" I mimicked his poor accent. He seemed out of place.

I moved on to the next person.

Mahi sat on top of the desks with her legs spread. I tried hard not to look in that direction. She had no clue how uncomfortable a guy like me could feel if a girl sat in that manner. Nevertheless, she was reading a very popular fashion magazine. On seeing me, she hid the picture of the near naked chick on the cover. "What do you want *smarty pants?"* she asked.

"Nothing Mahi. Just asking, how much have you studied?"

"I just completed five chapters out of ten," she replied. "Will complete the rest, once I am done with this magazine," she smiled harmlessly.

I nodded and moved ahead. Next was the topper of our class, Vaishali Sharma (my ex).

"Hi Vaishy! All ready to rock?" I asked joyously.

She started at me with tennis ball sized eyes for a good minute or so. "Did I say something offensive?" I clarified.

"No," she replied. "Just got lost in my thoughts," she added and looked into my eyes.

Strange, I said to myself and just ignored her and moved ahead.

My next victim was Pallu. Although that mini fight last day had strained our friendship, I just couldn't resist the pleasure of asking him, how *sex* had helped before exams. "Hey Pallvinder! All prepared?" I asked, deliberately not using his last name.

"Ritesh, I am sorry dude! I know I was wrong. I should have listened to you, forgive me dude! I am really sorry…" he started speaking bull shit as usual for which I showed him the centre finger.

"You were never wrong dude…sex helps in your testosterone levels…keep up the good work, keep it up!" I patted his back, full on with sarcasm and moved ahead in spite of his mild protests of not paying attention to the trash he had to say.

The last student I attended to was Aaru. My face lit up on seeing her and my heart beats increased.

"Hi," I said.

"Hey," she replied.

"Wassup? Prepared well enough eh?" I asked.

"Not really…" she shut the Political Science book to pay more attention to what I had to say.

"Same here just didn't find enough time," I chuckled.

"How would you? You were busy discussing sex weren't you?" she snapped.

I made a long face, "I was trying to show him the right path."

"Really? What makes you think that you were right and he wasn't?" she asked.

"The very reason that *you* supported me…" I answered her query. I sat down on top of her desk.

"But, I can be wrong. To make Pallu understand, you have to justify your statement," she said.

"Well, that is more or less simple… See, he already is apologizing. So, I guess things haven't gone as per plan, so I won!"

"No you haven't and neither will you. Unless and until you tell him why that sort of relation is not necessary," she explained.

"Do you know why?" I asked.

"Yes I do, but since you are his better friend, it is your duty to pass him that message. I know we over reacted last day," she agreed.

"See, to be emotionally bonded with someone takes more amounts of time and feelings. It is something that builds up and is best when we don't involve the physical aspect to it. You can get physical with anyone and anywhere…say…commercial sex workers. But, to be emotionally attached with someone takes a great deal and when something like that happens, it is there to stay," I lectured.

Aaru smiled, "I loved you. We were emotionally attached, did our relation last?"

"See, as far as I know, *this* line can never be disconnected...you know the one between you and me. Never!" I answered her innocently. She blushed.

She adjusted her hair clip, "So go and tell him where he went wrong and why it is important to make your partner earn physical intimacy rather than just give it to him or her on a platter. And secondly, tell him all that you lectured about the emotional factor being more important. I am glad to know that you think so deeply and so differently, just go and tell your friend that."

"Thank you dear, for sharing the same thoughts. I hate it when things get too superficial," I spoke softly.

"Now go and tell your friend what is right and what isn't before it is too late. And then don't come back to narrate me the entire thing, I don't want silly distractions. We have an exam today and day after is mathematics; so in all probability I will be meeting you today evening or tomorrow. We can discuss then...now go!" she stressed on the last word.

"Ok...bye," I got down from the desk, turned and was about to walk ahead when she held me back by my shirt.

"All the best stupid," she giggled as I turned to face her again.

"All the best to you too..." I wanted to tell her that I still loved her but was content with what I said.

Saniya glared at Pallu. Ritesh got apprehensive about what he had just spoken. There were a few stares that Saniya passed and all weren't pleasing.

"So you were physically involved with someone?" She asked.

Pallu chose not to answer.

"Well, he got ditched the very next day," Ritesh intervened.

"BUT STILL.....!" Saniya protested.

"Relax Saniya. I explained everything to Pallu, I did," Ritesh spoke again as Pallu looked on silently.

"Yes, he did," Pallu whispered. "I was always so scared of sex after that day on..." he murmured again.

"No wonder, you were acting so gay last time I was trying to seduce you...!" Saniya snapped.

Ritesh let out a cough to tell them about his presence. Saniya understood her mistake.

"I am sorry Saniya. I should have told you this, now please don't decide not to marry me..." Pallu folded his palms.

Saniya looked at him disdainfully.

"Yes, Saniya. Please don't refuse him now, at least you know him well enough now and he loves you a lot because of the very fact that he is afraid to lose you," Ritesh tried to make sense.

"But...still! I don't want to spend my life with someone who had sex when he was sixteen," Saniya argued.

"So what??! We all make mistakes don't we?" Ritesh asked.

Saniya kept quiet.

Ritesh decided to lighten up the mood a little. "You know Saniya, we generally have to pay loads and loads of extra money for types of coffee we can't even pronounce...sad nah?"

Pallu and Saniya chuckled.

"And also, did you see these new CD shrink covers? We will need a hacksaw to open them," Ritesh added.

Pallu and Saniya laughed, the mood lightened.

"Sorry..." Pallu said. "It's okay!" Saniya held his hands.

Ritesh smiled. "So should I continue?" he asked.

"Yes, please do..." Saniya exclaimed.

"It is day – minus one of the Mathematics pre boards. A tutor is worried for his student as it is the only way how his life can be good again," Ritesh narrated.

"Why only mathematics?" Saniya asked.

"Because Mathematics was the one big thing I helped Aaru with other than Science. So maybe sharing with you the incidents leading up to and after the mathematics exam can sum up the story quite well..."

"Aaru wanted good marks and you wanted her, right?" she asked.

"Yes. Absolutely. For that Mathematics and especially Thales had a lot in stake," Ritesh smiled.

"Continue..." Pallu spoke in between.

"Here I go..." Ritesh rubbed his palms and continued speaking.

The Final Meeting

"B.P.T, Pythagoras, Converse of Pythagoras, Similarity…" I read out the names of the different theorems.

Aaru sat next to me, ticking away all the names she was familiar and well versed with and was putting a question mark next to the ones she wasn't.

Once, I had read out all the theorems and formulaes in the entire syllabus, I looked up at her. She seemed so appealing. Her eyes glittered under the fading evening light and the soft wind blew her beautiful hair. She was wearing a white *kurti* and jeans and for a change she did away with those dangling earrings which I hated. She smiled on seeing that I was observing her so closely. Her cheeks formed those crevices called dimples and at that moment I promised myself that I would keep this girl smiling for the rest of her life. Just for that moment of bliss when I would get to see her dimples.

"All of them ready, stupid," she said.

I nodded, still lost in my world.

"What?" she asked.

"Nothing. I was worried about tomorrow's exam," I tried to misguide her thoughts.

It felt as though she had understood everything I had to say. "I am sad," she said.

"Why?" I asked back.

"I was beginning to enjoy your company lately…you know meeting you and all, it was fun," she pointed out.

I smiled, "Yes, it surely was. But, all things can't last forever can they? Someday or the other, we knew this would happen."

"I agree," she nodded. "But, nevertheless, I had a *bindaas* time…sir…!"

"Ha ha…now don't call me that after Mathematics is over tomorrow…" I fell silent. "Are you taking up *Mathematics* in 11?" I asked.

"If you promise to teach me…I would," she made this expression which made her so huggable.

"Wo! Not a chance," I said even though I wanted to do it.

"Fine, then I won't take up Mathematics," she made a sad face.

"Arre, 11 is very far off. Think of the boards dear…till the boards, I am definitely there to help you out," I patted her back.

"Thanks."

"Hmmm…*aur batao*…where do you go from here on?" I asked her.

"I go back home…change clothes…."

"No no! Not this, I meant life in general," I interrupted her.

"Oh, that *toh* I haven't decided. I might take up medicals as a choice of career…but again, it all depends on my boards."

"So, very true!"

"Hey stupid, what about you?"

"Hmmm…I want to pursue advertising as a career. *Yeh* engineering *aur* medicals, *meri bas ki baat nahi hai!*" I replied.

She laughed at my reply, "You will be a good ad filmmaker. You are creative and it will help surely."

"I hope so…maybe someday I will come to you for free medical checkups," I stated.

"Nothing's free in this world, my friend…!" she caressed her hair.

"Not even you for me??!"

She nodded her head in disapproval. I kept quiet till another question popped up.

"Hey Aaru!" I said.

"What?"

"How come you are so comfortable when you meet me in this park? Otherwise, at other places, you get so paranoid of meeting up with me. What's so special about this?"

"This actually is totally in the other direction of my house and is surrounded my individual housings. So, *my tons and tons of family friends and relatives* are generally restricted to the other side of the sector. Only once in a hundred times will you find them lurking around here. So, I am free to meet you here," she giggled. I saw no reason in doing that.

"I see, so we can meet up here at times?"

"What's the need to? We have the phone; I will call you at times…surely!"

I shrugged and decided to ask my next question, "What if you don't secure the Science batch, what'll happen then?"

"*Tamasha.* Mom and dad will break into tears, all my relatives will start comparing me to my brothers and you know the general Indian household drama..."

"Oh!"

"...And also they'll start pointing out major flaws in bringing me up and how I do this and how I do that and why I should be like my brothers and all...you know?"

I nodded and she continued, "Samarth bhaiyya cracked JEE recently. He got an All India Rank of 235. Isn't it amazing?"

"Oh yeah," I said even not knowing why the f*ck one needed ranks to do something he wanted to do for the rest of his life.

Aaru was in no mood to stop, "And Sarthak bhaiyya...he is pursuing computer sciences at IIT Bombay!"

I nodded again, knowing it very well that I would never be able to do something like that.

"I feel so proud of them at times...!" Aaru exclaimed.

"What about the guy who teaches you Mathematics? What do you think he will do in life?" I asked with a lot of directness involved.

"Umm...I can't comment on what he'll do but I can say this much that he will be successful in whatever he does. This is because he knows what is wrong and what is right and over the years he has learnt this art of following your heart without wasting your mind. And this is really the *bestest* part about you," in a state of over enthusiasm, she placed an arm around my neck and shook me apart.

"Nice nice..." I repeated my signature dialogue.

"And please don't forget me when you become an Ad guru...ok?"

she asked sweetly.

"Of course not…*stupid!*" I said.

We both laughed over it.

"I am tensed…" she said. "…I don't know about mathematics tomorrow, I was failing in it and now I am seeing dreams of scoring well," she looked here and there while speaking.

"That is perhaps the best part of seeing dreams," I said. "You just don't have to restrict yourself with anything, dreams are free and endless…." I added.

"I know…but heartbreaks too are for free," she stated.

"Yes they are but still, once you pursue your dreams, you actually achieve a part of it."

"Really? That is so nice to hear," she virtually clapped for what I had just said.

"And at times even if dreams seem to evade you, the feeling you get while trying to pursue it lasts you for a lifetime and all those dreams yet to be fulfilled seem very close all of a sudden," I held her hand and strangely, she didn't resist.

She placed another hand of hers on top of mine, "I know…I know…" she smiled.

The sun had set and the final lights of the day were the only thing to be seen.

"It's late," I pointed out. "You should be going back now…tomorrow is an important day for you…I will meet you in school," I added.

She nodded and stood up. She let go off my hand, "I won't say bye…it will give me more reasons to hope for a meeting tomorrow."

"Ha ha…nice dialogue," I chuckled.

"It came from the heart *stupid.* It did!" She said as I looked at her in awe just for the remaining seconds.

I didn't want her to leave me and go, but, I had no other choice. She was still not mine; she was still that eluding dream …

One Last Time

I stood in an atrium. I failed to recognize the place even though I could establish a direct connection with it. It was beautifully decorated.

The walls were covered with different sized portraits and each portrait had a story to tell. They were depicting my life, every single sphere of it.

My first car ride, my outings with mamu, my journey to the Victoria Memorial – everything was captured in the frames on one side. Then on the other side was the picture of me entering Montessori and then joining my school in Noida. There were other portraits as well. My first trophy, my first heart break, my first cycle, my first computer…everything had its well earned place in those portraits adorning the wall.

However, there was this one big portrait that caught my eye the most. It was that of Aaru and me. It depicted the scene when I first went to meet her at her apartments last year. It captured the expression of Aaru which I had failed to describe and also the elated me, nervous and excited at the same time.

A lanky framed teenager with a mobile in one hand and with his other hand on the handle of his cycle was racing through crowded streets. He had this grin of self belief and over achievement which was hard to take away from him. He knew that he wasn't wrong, not matter what people felt. He knew how important it was for him to reach his destination. He knew that someone waited for him.

From within the shadows of that particular frame, approached a young man in his mid thirties. He was decently dressed and his face was not visible clearly under the dim light. He approached me with cautiousness and spoke the moment he felt my attention, "Hi Ritesh, recognize me?"

"No," I replied. "I can't see your face properly," I put in.

"You will never be able to see my face because I don't exist," he said.

"Who are you?" I asked.

"I am you…I am what you will be twenty years from now," he spoke in a tone of assurance.

"Is this some joke?" I asked lamely.

"No Ritesh. It isn't…it is me who is talking to you, it is the 'face unseen' of yours that has come to meet you," his tone had a tinge of conviction and he stressed on certain words much like I did.

"Why can't I see your face?" I questioned.

"Because you don't know what your face will be, twenty years hence…" he answered.

"What do you mean?"

"I have come here to tell you about myself, I have come to tell you your future," he encircled me like a spirit; I still couldn't see his face.

"Why the future? Why not the past?" I asked.

"You know the past, don't you? That is the very reason why I have decorated the walls with portraits which will serve as remembrances."

"What do you have to say?"

"Men have come and gone but are yet to understand the meaning of love..." he started.

After a pause he spoke again, "Now look at me. I am Ritesh Garg, General Manager of a very big multinational firm. I got serious about my life after my tenth. I studied day and night and shut out everything. I did what the world asked me to and I won...I did. I reached the zenith which is far away from the reach of the common man."

I still hadn't understood the essence of his presence, "So is this my future?" I asked.

"Perhaps it is or perhaps it's not. Let me elaborate," he loosened the knot of his tie.

I nodded in approval.

"See, I may have achieved something what the common man can never dream of but I lost something as well..."

"What?"

"I lost Aarushi," he said with melancholy in his voice.

I raised an eyebrow and was about to answer when he started speaking again.

"You see...I left the dreams of Aarushi and decided to take up life in conventional sense. I let go off her and never desired to get her back, I believed in the saying that one should let go off the thing he loves because if it was meant to be his, it will come back. But I was wrong...!"

"You were?" I asked surprised.

"Yes indeed. I might be the Ritesh Garg who commands power in the office or the one everyone admires but I am a lost soul. I lost my life…I lost my love. I let her go when I shouldn't have," his tone softened.

"But, now girls must be crazy about you…big bucks…flashy cars…" I said.

"But the girl whom I want is not interested anymore. She has her own life…a life where she lives on with her family and is settled with what she could achieve and what she couldn't," he added.

He continued, "But me? I am not content. I am a lost person…I am a loser because I couldn't hold on to her when it mattered the most. I thought that she would come back when I had the initials GM against my name, but I was wrong. So was the world which conspired to keep me away from her…I gave in…I gave in!" "And now, when I have everything one can possibly want…I don't have my angel and I don't have happiness. My want of success put her importance aside and I regret that." His voice was croaky now.

I could feel his misery, "What do you want me to do?" I asked.

"Try to figure out this face…" he marched towards me. His face was blurry but the voice, I had heard it somewhere before.

"This is exactly what you'll be twenty years down the line…faceless! And you can't change this fact," he commanded.

"But…" he added. "…but, you can change the initials against your name. You can change the magnitude of success, you can bring in happiness, you can get rid of all the regrets…you can and by doing so… you will give *me* life, you will give your future…*life!*"

I looked on in disbelief.

"You can never know what I look like or what you'll look like in the next twenty years. But, you can know what you will be like and the decision is yours," he said. "I let her go thinking that success would be the only thing that would bring her back but I forgot that man is a thirsty animal, he goes wherever he can locate the oasis of love. Aarushi is not living as flamboyant a lifestyle as I am, but she is happy which I am not. Maybe, every morning when she wakes up...she ponders over the love story gone all wrong but she forgets immediately when her daughter walks up to her asking for breakfast. But look at me...I am *all alone*."

"Why are you telling me all this? I still love her...I do and I'd never leave her," I protested.

"I did! I did leave her when I was of your age and I am suffering now. She came back or she offered to come back, but I refused...I said that the time was wrong and I needed to be someone before I could take her back but then time moved on and I lost her to that lucky one," he whispered.

He turned his back to me and spoke, "You have worked very hard to get her back. And you have done this all with honest intentions and selflessly. You want her back don't you? And you will, just that don't do what I did...don't refuse or don't let others decide what you should do. Remember, twenty years down the line, when you will be *me*, the regrets will only be *yours* and no one else's."

I swam through his advices.

"*One last time,* I repeat what I just said. A life with little less money and a lot of love will be loads better than no life and no love with loads of money. Trust me."

"But, why do you tell me all this?"

"I tell you all this to warn you from not entering the bandwagon, you represent love and you will continue to do so, may your future be known to you and may my face...may your face be the one you *want to see...*"

I didn't respond.

"Good bye my past...good bye master Garg," saying this, he vanished.

My mobile phone beeped twice. Someone had sent me a text message at four in the morning. The number was Aaru's father's:

'Hey sir! Just was thinking about you. I am revising. You also do the same. Imp day. All the best and gud monnin. (dnt reply)'

I smiled. *Thank God, the message came after the dream,* I said to myself. It'd be a pity if the dream had been interrupted...not everyday do you get to see your future. I prayed that all that Ritesh Garg had said was non-fiction...because if it was then I would definitely take his advices *seriously.*

Because You Loved Me

A couple of weeks later…

I was nervous…hell nervous.

I clicked the link twice… 'Error on Page', it blinked. *Oh God! What the f**k!* I tried again and my attempt was in vain…the same message flashed again. *Grrr…*

So, I paced the floors of my room…up and down, juggling the million pessimistic thoughts. Since morning, I had been trying hard to open the school site to view Aaru's marks but all this was to no avail. It was not that I was unhappy with what had been offered to me, the brilliant marks in Mathematics, Social Sciences and English were really looking good; but – I was honestly, super pissed with the fact that I still hadn't got to know Aaru's marks. The moment I entered her roll number on our school website, this bloody error message troubled me.

I was getting restless. I grabbed hold of the water bottle kept in my room and started drinking water…I drank on till I emptied it. The giddy sensation did not help a bit. I sat down and started contemplating.

I had put in my heart and soul while teaching Aaru, I put in more effort than it was required. She too had done a good job in using all that I had to offer. Those tireless nights of teaching constantly reminded me of the disappointment I might had to face or maybe she would…if incase, her results were not good. If incase, her science marks were not in the nineties and her mathematics was not in the upper eighties. Then, in all probability she would be in the toughest situation of her life. Those six or eight genius baboons she had as her cousins would be a benchmark for her and would constantly remind her that she is a failure. And, in ninety nine cases out of hundred, my lectures on philosophy would not help matters.

And more so, she hadn't yet agreed on whether we would reunite or not…she had this lame *I don't know* kind of attitude whenever we spoke about loving each other or anything of that sort.

I violently took out my phone from the drawer and dialed her number. I forgot that we were not supposed to speak to each other, I forgot for a moment that she had a dangerous lioness in the form of her mother – all I wanted to know was the outcome. I wanted to know whether she emerged victorious or not. I wanted to know whether we had risen together or not. And in this urge of knowing things, I dialed her previous mobile number which was out of service these days. I kept on trying that number till my phone's battery retired. I took in a deep breath.

I entered her roll number again…and yet again there was this same old response. Freaking errors…*why only her page*, I thought.

After a while, there was a knock on the door. "Yes," I answered.

"There is a call for you…" Mom said.

"Who? Tell him that I am busy…" I replied lazily.

"It's Aarushi."

"What did you say?" I jumped up, suddenly I was drowning in a pool of Gatorade.

"I said that it is Aarushi…" Mom said impatiently.

"Then why are you wasting time…give it to me…" I rushed up to the door, snatched the phone from her hands and closed the door on her face (which was very rude).

"Hullo." I said.

"Hi…" she replied.

"What?"

"Nothing stupid, can't I call you…just like that?"

"Well…no…but what about your marks…?" "Did you get to open the site? Here it's showing errors."

"Hmm…papa got my marks from the school office – in the morning itself." Her voice gave me a feeling that she was crying. I could have been wrong.

"Is everything alright?"

"I don't know." She replied.

"Aaru, c'mon…don't start off again!"

"Forget it…can you meet me today?"

"Sure…" I said without a doubt.

"Okay, meet me near the Block-A Park. I want to see you sharp at four thirty."

"So early? What's the hurry? Tell me your marks…!"

"Don't argue…just do what I say! I have enough on my plate

already – please listen to me." She tried to convince.

"Aaru…is your result good or bad? …itna toh batao!" I felt helpless.

"I TOLD YOU! STOP ASKING THE SAME OLD QUESTION! Just meet me in the evening will you?"

"Fine…as you wish!" I didn't like her croaky voice and I expected the outcome to be bad.

"Bye…" she said.

"Bye bye."

Early in the evening at around four thirty…the park was empty. Most of the people were enjoying the afternoon nap. And I was a bit circumspect to the idea of meeting at desolate places. As I approached the entrance of the park…I saw Aaru sitting on a bench. On seeing me, she stood up and walked towards me.

She was wearing a colourful jumper and her hair was tied properly. She was wearing a pair of denim jeans and the colour combinations suited her perfectly. There was this hint of exuberance that appealed to me the most that particular evening.

When she came closer, I noticed that her eyes weren't looking perfect. I guessed it right in the morning…she was crying.

When we were at an arms distance, she stopped.

"Ritesh…can I hug you?"

"Whoa?" I couldn't believe what I had heard.

"What whoa? Do I need to take permission to hug you?" she asked.

"Hug…permission…yes…I mean no…but why…marks?" I didn't know where to begin.

"Tell me something stupid, why are you so interested in knowing my marks?" she said.

"Dunno…" I replied. My eyes were tennis ball sized.

"Ok…I need to tell you something. But before that can you tell me something?"

"Whoa? I mean what?" I replied.

"How do people hug? As in…does the girls' arm go around the neck of the boy or beneath his arms?"

"Why do you ask me this?" I replied, still subconscious to the proceedings.

"You must have had the habit of hugging girls while I was away." She spoke in sarcastic sense.

"No. Never tried that. Girls seldom interested me other than you."

"Oh that's good. Since you don't know how to hug and same with me…why not…"

"Why not what?" I didn't allow her to complete the sentence.

"When will you learn to shut up?" She asked and said at the same time.

She came closer to me and slung her arms around my neck…as though it was Newton's third law of motion – I held her almost immediately.

And then, unknowingly…perhaps for the first time…we were in each other's arms. We held onto each other as long as we could – and for the first time, Aaru wasn't afraid of whether there were people around. She didn't find what we were doing as *ajeeb* …I held her close to my heart, tight and warm. All the miseries we had shared trickled down our hearts and vanished into thin air as we held onto each other.

We let go of each other after good long five minutes or so which felt like eternity. A drop of tear rolled down her cheek; I wiped it gently. She had no reason to cry, "Don't cry…" I said.

"I am with you and we will face it again…" I continued.

"Face what?" She asked, concerned.

"You didn't manage to get proper marks, right? Don't worry there is always a next time."

"Shut up idiot….I topped in Mathematics and I beat you in Science by five marks…!" she exclaimed.

"What???! You topped? You got ninety two in Science…are you serious?" I couldn't control my joy on hearing this. She had actually achieved what she had to. No longer would her parents bother her and all that had been lost had now been repaired. Both of us had fallen together and by God's wishes we rose together as well. It seemed a dream come true for me and that point of time…there were no words that could do justice to my feelings.

"YES!" She seemed ecstatic.

"You disappointed me…I expected a thirty three or a thirty four from you…" I said in an artificially morose tone

"Idiot…!" She kicked me. *Bam* on my shin…it hurt.

"Ouch!" I cried out.

I guess she enjoyed the feel of hugging for the first time and so did I. So she pulled me and we held onto each other again for quite some time.

"Because you loved me…I don't mind falling in love…all over again!" she said as we both shared a good laugh over it.

She was still in my arms and I was in hers…

Some stories are meant to have happy endings. And so did mine.

Ritesh finished the last sentence and lifted the glass of water. Saniya lost it completely as she jumped out of her chair and smothered Ritesh with wet kisses all over his face.

"You did it…you did it…you did it…you did it…you got her back!!" she shouted out.

"HEY GUYS! RITESH GOT AARU BACK!" She screamed in joy. The other diners got irritated at first but later on, seeing this over excited girl…all of them sported a nice smile.

It took Ritesh and Pallu and a little bit of stern advices from the management to calm Saniya down.

Finally when she was seated, Ritesh spoke, "All's well that ends well…!"

"Yes…"Pallu let out a sigh of relief.

"Yes, absolutely! YEIPPPPEEEEEEEEE I STILL CANT BELIEVE IT!" Saniya joyously exclaimed.

Ritesh grinned from ear to ear.

"Are you publishing this?" Saniya asked.

"No…why?" Ritesh rpelied.

"You should…it would be…" she was about to say something when a stranger approached the table.

She was young and beautiful and was wearing a very well embroidered kurti and jeans. Her eyes were blue black and long lashed. Saniya stared at her for a long time and so did Pallu. Ritesh had his back turned to her.

On seeing both of them staring at her, all confused, she smiled. Two beautiful dimples were formed on her cheeks on both sides.

Feeling someone's presence, Ritesh turned around to see who it was. The colour of his face changed completely. His eyes started glittering again and his heart started beating faster. He stood up almost immediately to greet her and introduce her, "Hi. So you are late…" he showed her the watch.

"Guys, let me introduce you to her, she is…" Ritesh was about to take that girl's name when Saniya stood up violently to interrupt him.

"JUST SHUT UP JUST SHUT UP!" she shouted out. Ritesh fell silent.

She then spoke sweetly, "Let me introduce her…" Saniya said.

Ritesh nodded.

"Ladies and gentlemen, boys and girls, presenting before you…the one and only…Aarushi…" Saniya announced. People turned to looked at the tamasha going on.

"Yes, yes and she is my…" Ritesh began to speak again. And again he was cut short by Saniya.

"Yes, yes..we know that already…she is your angel…she is your miracle!" Saying this, she broke into laughter; the other three followed her cue.